A
Conflict
of
Interest

A RINEHART SUSPENSE NOVEL

A RINEHART SUSPENSE NOVEL

A
CONFLICT
OF
INTEREST

Brad Williams

AND

J. W. Ehrlich

HOLT, RINEHART AND WINSTON
New York   Chicago   San Francisco

Published simultaneously in Canada by Holt, Rinehart and Winston of Canada, Limited.

Library of Congress Catalog Number: 78-138869

First Edition

ISBN: 0-03-086020-2

Printed in the United States of America

A
Conflict
of
Interest

A RINEHART SUSPENSE NOVEL

1

*A*s THE PLANE descended over the water on its straight-in approach to the airport, the wing dipped slightly, and he glimpsed the mistletoe-gray streamers of fog curling over the south San Francisco hills. It could have been the same fog there when he left more than five years ago, and he thought it unlikely that the city had changed much. He was the one who had changed. When he had left, he had been clean-shaven. His suit had been conservatively tailored. He could not remember what kind of shoes he had been wearing—probably the same uniform black as the five men wore who were seated in the same row of seats. He combed his pepper-and-salt beard with his fingers. One thing was certain; he had not been wearing the Mexican *guaraches* on his feet.

The stewardess came by and told him impolitely to restore his seat to the upright position. "Have I been riding in it upside down?" he asked.

The man next to him laughed, but the girl didn't hear him. She had moved on down the aisle. The wings wobbled again, and he saw the bay below him. It was covered with whitecaps, and as the plane flared out for the touchdown, he saw spray from the bay leap over the rocks of the breakwater. No, the weather had not changed; fog in the city and the wind blowing like hell at the airport.

The plane stopped at the jetway, and he bent over and pulled out the compact Samsonite suitcase from beneath the seat, then rose and adjusted his poncho. The suitcase was relatively new, and it contrasted oddly with the Mexican clothes he wore.

"It's probably full of smack," one stewardess said to another as he passed their frozen smiles on the way out of the aircraft. He knew the remark was directed toward him, but he did not understand it, and he was not sufficiently interested to ask for a translation. He felt sorry for them, and then the idea occurred to him that they might have the same feeling toward him.

In the finger foyer he paused and looked around, but could find no familiar face. He turned and walked down a long corridor, and stepped on the moving walk. And then he heard a voice over the public address system paging Cyrus Thurman to a white courtesy telephone. It had been so long since he had heard his name pronounced with an English accent rather than Spanish that he did not recognize it for a moment. It made little difference. There is no white courtesy telephone on a moving sidewalk.

When the sidewalk ended, he continued down another passageway into the central section of the airport and entered the large central foyer. This had been refurbished since he left. Ticket counters for some of the old airlines had disappeared. New ones had been added. It looked better, but it occurred to him that airports were becoming no more than bus stations. The excitement of an airport was gone. He strolled over to a newsstand and glanced at the headlines. These had not changed. An Army general, speaking before the Commonwealth Club, had stated that the war in Vietnam had made a turn toward complete victory. A Black Panther had been killed in a shoot-out. The University Board of Regents had found another Communist at Berkeley.

"Hello, Dad."

He turned around and held out his arms. "Junior!" he cried, embracing him, and then pushing him away to hold him at arm's length to study him. The youth wore his hair long, but was clean-shaven except for bushy sideburns. His face seemed slightly effeminate.

"I almost didn't recognize you with the beard and, you know," the boy said. He ran his hands through his hair. "They were paging you."

"I heard, but I couldn't find a telephone. You look great." He dropped his arms, picked up the suitcase, adding, "It probably was Albert."

"He's a real pain in the ass."

Thurman laughed. "That's no way to speak of your step-brother." They started toward the main exit. "He tells me you're a hippie."

"Yeah, I know."

"I tried to call your sister from Los Angeles also, but there was no answer."

"Sometimes Raquel works late. She's all for making money."

"Is she a pain in the ass also?"

Junior laughed. "That's a put-on, Dad. Raquel's great. I went by the store and told her you were coming. She says to come out to her house right away."

"Albert asked me to stay with him."

"He would try and make you shave and cut your hair and buy a suit. He just got promoted to lieutenant colonel."

Now Thurman laughed. "Okay, I'll call him from Raquel's."

They went out of the terminal building and turned toward the distant parking area. There was an unaccustomed chill in the air, and he shivered under the woolen poncho. He had lived in the tropics so long that his blood was thinned. Junior, wearing only a faded blue shirt and thin pants, appeared perfectly comfortable. The wind blew scraps of paper and swirls of dust along the sidewalk, forcing him to move with his head down, and so he did not see the car Junior was driving until he was next to it. Then he stepped back and stared at it curiously. Not even in Mexico would a person drive a vehicle painted in such a manner.

It was an ancient Volkswagen bus. The rear windows were covered from the inside with old "McCarthy for President" posters barely distinguishable through the splatters of paint on the windows. The area from the back of the front seat forward was painted a fire-engine red. The remainder of the bus was covered by every possible color. He got the impression that cans of paint had been opened and thrown against the side of the vehicle, and that after it dried, someone then had pasted hundreds of flower decals over it. Junior made no comment, took his suitcase, and tossed it in a side door on top of a couple of mattresses on the floor, then walked around the car and climbed up behind the wheel.

Although it was early for the rush-hour-traffic peak, the cars they faced on the freeway were barely crawling. He knew that by the time they reached the city, they would become enmeshed not only in traffic crossing the Golden Gate Bridge, but by fog as well.

"How long are you going to be?" Junior asked. He drove at a moderate speed in the right lane.

"Just a few days. I've got to be back next week for a special fishing trip to Manzanillo."

"I'd like to come down and visit you."

"Come back with me if you want."

Junior reached over and touched him affectionately on the

arm. At the same moment, a heavy gust of wind slammed into the left side of the bus, pushing it from the freeway onto a dirt shoulder. Junior pulled it back on the pavement and then slowed.

"Why don't you get something a little lower to the road?" Thurman asked.

The boy laughed. "It's not mine. I just borrowed it, you know."

"You mean it's hot?"

The bus swayed off the pavement two more times in the heavy wind, until they passed Candlestick Park and entered the fog. "How's your painting coming?" the man asked.

"Pretty good. I sold one a little while ago, and I've got a couple in a gallery in Carmel."

"Are you becoming a commercial artist?"

The boy shook his head. "No way," he replied, "unless you go broke."

"Good for you. You should come down to Mexico for a different influence. There's plenty of room."

"Maybe I will. I got in a bad scene around here."

"Bad trouble?"

"No. It's moved on."

The man nodded. "You ever need help, go see Sam Benedict."

"The lawyer?"

"Is there another one?"

The fog became dense, and it took almost two hours to creep across the city and over the Golden Gate Bridge. The moment they entered Marin County on the northern edge of the bridge, the fog lifted. Turning, Thurman could see the upper portions of the tall buildings on the hills of San Francisco piercing the cloud layer. In the dimming light, it left an eerie effect of a city floating in the air, and he remarked upon it.

"It's a city floating on pot," Junior said as he turned off the freeway into the narrow winding road that curled along the edge of the bay into Sausalito. In the center of the town, he waved to a bearded trio crossing the street in front of him, then turned left and climbed a tortuous hill that twisted its way up the side of the mountain. A short time later, he pulled the bus onto a platform built out of the side of the hill adjacent to a flat single-story house supported partially by stilts. A small Porsche coupé was parked in front of the bus, and they had to sidle their way past this before they could reach the steps that led down to the dwelling.

Raquel opened the door before they reached it and leaped up a couple of steps to embrace him. Dropping his suitcase, Thurman hugged her happily, kissed her, then followed her into the house. In the soft light of the comfortably furnished living room, he felt a slight shock as he saw her. The difference between twenty and twenty-five was remarkable. When he left, she had been a girl, mature and rounded, but still a girl. Now she was all woman. Her hair was jet black, which was not her natural color, and it hung loosely down her back, caught at the nape of the neck by a gold barrette. Her blouse was made of a material that looked like snakeskin, and from the way her full breasts moved loosely beneath it, he knew she wore no bra. Her pants were tight in the crotch and flared out over the ankles.

"Come on, Daddy," she teased. "I'm your daughter."

He grinned. "Then pour me a Scotch," he replied. "And tell me who is keeping you."

"I play the field." Her laugh was happy, like tiny bells ringing. "Why didn't you let us know you were coming earlier?"

Thurman took off his small sombrero, and then raised the poncho over his head. "I didn't decide to come until last night. I tried to call you from Los Angeles during the stopover." He took the glass of Scotch from her and sank down into a comfortable sofa. "I reached Albert and Junior, but couldn't raise you."

"Getting hold of Junior is something else again," she agreed, sitting down Indian style on the floor in front of him. "How did you ever manage that?"

"I had a feeling, so I answered the phone," Junior said. "Sometimes I get real strong feelings."

Raquel reached out and held Thurman's hand in both of hers. "You're not going back in business, are you? You'll have to shave, and that beard is right out of Hemingway."

"No. Just a small affair that I must take care of."

"If it's just small, that's good. I'll take tomorrow off and drive you around. Or I'll take a week off."

"You don't have to do that, Quel. I've just got to see Sam Benedict."

"You kill someone?"

Again he laughed. "It's a personal matter." He finished his Scotch and passed the empty glass to Raquel. "I'll have another," he said, and struggled to his feet. The sofa was very low and difficult to manipulate. "And while you are making it, I'll call Albert."

"Oh, God," Raquel said, rising as effortlessly as a yoga teacher. "He and Althea are more insufferable now than when you were here."

"If they bug you, don't see them."

"I don't very often." She walked over to a small bar, hips swinging. "But lately he has had a thing against Junior. He wants him to join the Army and straighten out."

"No kidding, Dad. That's what he said," Junior agreed. He pointed toward the window. "The telephone is in a box over there."

There was only one box on a small table near the window, and when Thurman raised the lid, he found the telephone inside of it. He dialed the number, then looked outside the window. When there was no fog, the view surely must be magnificent, but now the city had disappeared. Only the Sausalito waterfront was visible, and the fog was already licking the ends of the piers and had half-swallowed the old ferry that was permanently moored to the dock.

Someone with a Swedish accent answered the telephone. "Colonel Albert Thurman's residence."

"Tell the Colonel that the General would like to speak to him, please."

"Yes, sir."

A moment later Albert came on the telephone. "Yes, sir," he said deferentially.

"Congratulations on your promotion."

There was a brief pause. "Father?" the Colonel asked. There was a stiffness in his voice, and the elder Thurman smiled as he pictured his oldest son holding the telephone with a frown creasing his face. "I tried to reach you at the airport earlier. Did you come on a later flight?"

"No. Junior met me. I'm at Raquel's."

"Althea and I were expecting you here. We have a room prepared."

"Thank you, but I'm already unpacked. I'm going to take the kids out to dinner. I have an appointment tomorrow with my attorney, and I can drop by midmorning on the way. Perhaps tomorrow night." Raquel came over to him, raised up on her toes, blew in his ear, and handed him a fresh Scotch.

"I'm sitting on a court-martial at eight thirty."

"Then I'll see you tomorrow night."

Again the Colonel paused. "I think there is something you should know before you see your attorney," he said presently. "It is important."

"Then I'll come over after dinner, somewhere around ten or eleven."

"I'll pick you up at ten."

"There's no need. I'll have Junior or Quel drive me over."

"I prefer that Junior not be seen around this neighborhood, Father."

"Very well, Albert," the elderly Thurman replied. "I'll drive myself over in Junior's red wagon." He replaced the telephone in its box, then closed the lid. "I'm inclined to agree with you children," he said, walking back to the sofa. "In some ways, Albert is a most perplexing man."

"He thinks I've got a hang-up," Junior said quietly. "But he and Althea are the ones with a hang-up."

Raquel laughed. "I have cheap wine, discounted Scotch, and I'm a terrible cook, and so all three of us will probably wind up with a hangover, but we're all going to eat right here."

"You're my favorite daughter."

"You can say that because I'm your only one," she replied.

"You're all my children."

"Even Albert?" Junior asked wryly.

Thurman nodded. "Even Albert," he said.

It was almost eleven when Cyrus Thurman left the house on the hill in Sausalito. Junior wanted to drive him back into San Francisco, and then Raquel had wanted to, but when he insisted he drive alone, they did not persist. Handling the vividly colored bus was easy. He let it roll down the steep hill in low gear into the central part of the village. At the traffic light, three bearded young men and a couple of long-haired girls passed in front of him and waved. He waved back. He was in uniform as much as Albert.

The fog hit him at the northern edge of the Golden Gate Bridge, flooding in from the ocean pass to the huge bay, and he rolled down the window, pushed out his head, and concentrated on the yellow dividing lines on the highway. It was a good feeling to drive in the fog and be a little bit drunk in San Francisco again. Soon he caught up with some bright taillights, and he followed these easily to the toll booth. This, he noted, was different. Instead of the usual twenty-five cents, the toll now was fifty cents for cars heading south and free to those traveling north. The toll collector looked at him, then shook his head and waved him past.

Albert and Althea lived in the Marina District of San Francisco in an expensive house near the Presidio and the Golden Gate. From the second floor of their home, one could see the spires of the bridge. Before he had left, Thurman remembered, the room with the best view of the bridge had been turned into a den by Althea, and it was here that she preferred to entertain, or go through the ritual of what she called entertainment. She would probably offer him a sherry. But if she smelled the Scotch, she would give him nothing more than coffee.

This part of San Francisco did not appear to have changed much, although it was difficult to tell because of the fog. There was the same parking area by the seawall where he always had parked when he came to visit Albert, because neither his son nor his neighbors liked to find a bumper stretching even an infinitesimal fraction of an inch over their driveways. In the fog, he missed the entrance to the parking area, backed up as soon as he realized his error, then cautiously groped the noisy Volkswagen into the lot. He looked to his left, and then braked abruptly, stopping only inches away from a sedan. A young girl in the rear seat bolted upright, at the same time pulling a sweater down over her breasts.

"Sorry," he called out as he backed away. He eased the bus around the rear of the sedan, cautiously drove a few yards, turned to the right, and came to a halt as the front of the car gently bumped the seawall. The thought occurred to him that he had not forgotten how to drive in a San Francisco fog.

It seemed abnormally quiet with the engine shut off. For a moment he listened fondly to the music of the foghorns in the bay. He could even hear the water lapping against the hulls of the boats tied up in the Yacht Club, invisible, but somewhere directly ahead. For perhaps a minute he listened to this concert; then he became aware of footsteps on the pavement behind him. The steps moved in a fast, even cadence, metal cleats on heels clicking across the macadam. They drew closer, then stopped abreast of the Volkswagen.

Cyrus Thurman pushed his head out of the open window and looked back. He was aware of a faint movement by the side of the vehicle before a tremendous blow struck him on the forehead, slamming him back inside of the bus. He slid from his seat after his head struck the doorjamb, but he did not know it. He was dead before his body came to a rest on the floor.

2

---

*T*HE TWO LOVERS were frozen in a wild, quick fear at the sound of the gunshots so near to them. First there had been one, and a quarter of a minute later, a second, and then they both heard the metal heel cleats rapidly slapping the pavement, coming toward them. The girl recovered first and pushed her lover away. He responded by rolling in one well-coordinated movement over the back of the front seat to a sitting position behind the steering wheel.

The car was new, and the engine started instantly. He backed it up, tires screeching on the pavement, across the sidewalk, over the curb, and onto the street. He braked abruptly, pulled the gear lever into the drive position, and screamed off blindly into the fog. Less than a block distant, he sideswiped a parked car with a heavy crunch. Instinctively he braked, and the engine stalled. Somewhere in back of him a woman screamed once, and then the cry was cut off. He turned the key, and the engine caught again. A dozen blocks away, he stopped the car again and adjusted his clothing. The girl climbed over the seat and pulled up a pair of panties under her skirt.

"Someone got killed," she said, her voice little more than a whisper.

"Maybe it was just someone shooting," the boy said, wetting his lips. He did not believe his explanation, but it was an answer.

"You smashed the car."

"Yeah. I don't think my father will be mad."

"Mine'd kill me. Did you hear that scream?"

"Yeah."

"Think we ought to call the cops?"

"We didn't see anything. We just heard." He looked at the clock on the dashboard. Eleven fifty. He was supposed to be home by midnight. "But I can call them from a pay phone and tell them what we heard."

"With those shots, he must be dead."

"I'll call from a service station."

"Yeah." The girl slid closer to him as he slowly moved down the street. "I read that if you only talk for a very short time, they can't trace the call." She put her arm through his. "Jesus, this is scary."

It took him a quarter of an hour to find a restaurant on Van Ness Avenue that was open. The girl wanted to go in with him, but when the door on her side would not open, she changed her mind.

When he returned, he inspected the damaged side of the car under the parking-lot lights, and when he slid under the wheel, she noticed that his face was very somber. "Bad?" she asked.

He nodded. "I really creamed it."

Shortly after midnight, Lieutenant Lars Burton of the Homocide Division of the San Francisco Police Department pulled up beside two police cars with flashing red lights near the seawall adjacent to the San Francisco Yacht Club. Burton was a short man, balding, and with a protruding stomach that seemed to ache constantly. He probably was the best detective in the San Francisco Police Department, and he would have enjoyed a much higher rank in the department had he been more politically oriented and less resistant to regulations he considered foolish.

Stepping out of his unmarked police car, he walked over to a uniformed officer standing beside the open door of a garishly painted Volkswagen bus. He looked inside and saw the body lying face down on the floor of the vehicle. The hand, stretched out on the seat, was that of an older man, although his hair and dress were hippie style. A green woolen garment was bunched around the body's shoulders. In the rear pants pocket, the bulge of a wallet was clearly outlined. Bending over, Burton worked the wallet loose, then directed the uniformed man to shine his flashlight on it as he opened the leather folder. It was a jacket-style wallet, which meant that the trouser pocket had been tailored much deeper than normal in order to hold it.

Inside were ten Mexican one-thousand-peso notes and five United States one-hundred-dollar bills, a ticket on Mexican Airlines between Los Angeles and Puerto Vallarta made out in the name of Cyrus Thurman, and a folded letter written on heavy rag-content bond. The heading on the stationery read:

> Sam Benedict
> Attorney at Law
> 100 Montgomery Street
> San Francisco, California

The letter was brief:

Dear Cy,
    Of course I shall be delighted to see you. The time
is fine.

    Burton refolded the letter and replaced it in the wallet. "Have
someone wake up Gus Corona and tell him Sam Benedict is involved
in this one." He gestured toward the bus. "Who belongs to this
junk?"
    "The registration is being checked now. It's last year's so
they are having a little problem."
    The detective nodded, and taking the flashlight from the uni-
formed man, he leaned inside the bus again. It was then that he noticed that a large square piece had been cut out from the green
woolen garment, and he swore softly as he straightened up once
again. "It looks like the Astro killer," he said to the uniformed man,
who now was in the front seat of the prowl car talking into a microphone. This information also was relayed. "Where's your partner
and the other team?"
    "Looking around," the officer replied.
    "We need about three more cars if we are going to hunt
around," Burton said, and he went back to his car. It would do little
good to block off the area. The pyscho got away even when there
was no fog. This cloud blanket would give him additional security.
Another car arrived, carrying a fingerprint detail. Next came the
crew from the coroner's office, and this modest hearse was quickly
followed by several more prowl cars, which arrived with sirens on,
and red roof lights muffled by the fog.
    It was after one thirty when Gus Corona appeared. Burton
watched as he slid out of the car and with the ease of a professional
athlete walked over to the VW. He glanced inside, then came over
to Burton. Corona was a political cop. He knew all of the important
people in the city, was well educated, young, and well liked. He possibly could wind up as chief. While several of the detectives resented
reporting to a younger man, Lars Burton was not among them.

"We received a call from some kid who wouldn't identify himself, that there had been a shooting here," Burton said, passing over the wallet he had taken from the dead man. "A piece of the dead man's shawl has been scissored out, so the newspapers will probably be getting a gift-wrapped package tomorrow or the next day."

"This makes eight, doesn't it?"

"Maybe nine, if you count that one in San Jose."

"Okay." Corona shrugged. "You've been doing most of the work on him. Why did you call me?"

Burton nodded toward the wallet Corona held in his hand. "Sam Benedict is involved, and I know he's a friend of yours." He pulled out a roll of peppermint-flavored antacid tablets from his pocket and popped one in his mouth as Corona opened up the wallet and took out the letter. Burton did not know Sam Benedict, although he had seen him on several occasions and had found him somewhat of an enigma. The attorney was taller than Corona and powerfully built. When he spoke, his voice was always soft and articulate and his manner relaxed. Only in these things was he consistent. On one occasion, when Burton had seen him in court, Benedict had been absolutely ruthless in his cross-examination of a hostile witness. Yet with another witness he had been as gentle and charming as a professional confidence man preparing to move in on a senile heiress. On still another occasion, he had seen the attorney on a talk television show. The host was renowned for his large vocabulary and delighted in verbally torturing his guests. But with Sam Benedict he more than met his match. It was the host who eventually slammed his fist on the table and stormed off the stage, while Sam Benedict, sprawled in his chair with an ankle on his knee, sincerely apologized to the viewers for upsetting the man who made a living out of insults.

Corona folded the letter back into the wallet and said, "If that is Thurman's body and he is a friend of Sam Benedict's, we're in for more publicity than usual. Thanks for calling me."

"How did you get to know Sam Benedict?"

"I met him at the club where I play tennis. He beats me most of the time."

"That's good politics," Burton said.

Corona shrugged. "It's not because I let him."

One of the uniformed policemen came over to the car. "There might be a couple of things you'll want to see," he said deferentially and led them with his flashlight, like an usher in a theater, to an area about fifty yards on the other side of the bus, where he pointed out the tire skid marks on the pavement. "He left in a hell of a hurry," the cop said. "He went straight back over the curb."

"We don't know when this was done," Burton said, "but have some pictures made of it when the fog lifts."

"There's a car that's been sideswiped down the street."

The three men walked down to it. The damaged car was a white late-model Lincoln. Its side had been creased near the rear, and then, as the dent approached the front, the metal of the body had been punctured. At the doorjamb they saw two car-door handles, one that belonged to the car and the other obviously torn off the car that struck it. From the door to the hood, the Lincoln was dented and smeared with either blue or black paint.

"We have some molding and a hubcap from the car that hit it," the cop said. "We can send them to the lab for identification."

Corona nodded. "Who belongs to the Lincoln?"

The uniformed cop pointed to a house behind them. "A Thomas Lancaster. That's where he lives."

The house was dark, and Burton suddenly realized that all the houses were dark. No one had stuck his head out to see what the red lights were about. No one had called to report gunfire except the youth. No one had called in to report a hit-and-run accident. The boy might live farther down the street, closer to the shooting, and possibly did not hear the accident. "If this is the Astro killer, we may have a hell of a break," Corona said. "Have all the garages notified. Get this heap towed in for study before Mr. Lancaster can get it to a garage."

The uniformed man nodded and went back to his prowl car. Strobe lights from cameras began flashing back at the VW bus. It would take at least a couple of hours before they would leave. First the body would go in the coroner's hearse. Then the police wreckers would take away the VW and the Lincoln. By morning, the only probable visible signs of the incident would be the tire marks.

Burton stuffed his pipe with tobacco as they slowly walked back to their cars. "This is the first time the psycho has ever spooked," he said.

Corona looked at his companion. "Go on," he said.

"It's my impression that he's been trying to get caught. On two occasions, according to his letters, he's waited around until we come. What would frighten him this time? Frighten him so much that he hot-rodded it over a curb and smashed into another car?" Burton puffed on his pipe. "Of course, that's assuming that our psycho was driving the car that hot-rodded it over the curb."

"Either way, we're ahead," Corona replied. "If it wasn't the psycho, then it was a witness."

"A witness in this fog?" Burton replied.

Corona laughed shortly. "I'll leave it to you," he said. "I'm going over to Pacific Avenue and wake up Sam Benedict."

The doorbell chimed, and Sam woke instantly. He flipped on the closed-circuit television by his bed and smiled when he recognized Gus Corona facing directly into the hidden lens of the television camera. Then his smile faded as he rapidly sifted through his mind the names of possible clients whose activities might prompt a visit at this time of night from a lieutenant attached to the Homicide Division. Corona pressed the call button once again.

"There's no one here," Sam said softly into the microphone.

18

"It's important, Sam."

The attorney pressed the button that released the door lock, returned to the bedroom, slipped into a robe, then went into the bathroom and splashed some water on his face. He went back to the penthouse living room and glanced at the two bronzed arms of the built-in wall clock. It was two forty-five in the morning. A muted bell sounded to announce that the private elevator had reached the top floor. He went out to the foyer and pressed another button that released the lift door.

"It's harder to get in here than a maximum-security cell," the detective said, stepping out of the elevator onto the thick carpet, "but it is a little more comfortable."

"It's easier to get out of," Sam replied, motioning the detective into the living room. "Would you like a drink?"

"A thin Scotch if you can afford it."

"Most of my clients pay their fees." He went over to the bar and poured a drink for his guest. Corona apparently had been roused from bed, he noticed, because of the heavy stubble of his dark beard. "And most of them are happy to pay."

Corona accepted the drink and sat down in a large easy chair. "You're big enough and strong enough to make them act like they are happy, at least." He rested an ankle on his knee. "Do you know a Cyrus Thurman?"

"Why do you ask?"

"It was a poor question," Corona said. "I have read a very brief letter you wrote to him, and I know you had an appointment with him at eleven this morning."

Sam's eyes narrowed slightly before he replied. "If you have been reading my correspondence and refer to Cy Thurman in the past tense, I presume this is the reason for your visit."

"Yeah. You can cancel the appointment." Corona sipped his drink. "There hasn't been any official identification yet, but at the moment we are assuming the body is that of Cyrus Thurman because of the papers found on the body. Can you describe Thurman?"

"I haven't seen him for five or six years, Gus. Gray hair, cut short, high cheekbones, a Dick Tracy jaw. He always dressed conservatively and expensively. What happened to him?"

"Looks like the Astro got to him, but the description doesn't match. This guy had a beard, long hair, wore Mexican clothes, even to the shoes."

"Could be," Sam said thoughtfully. "He's been living in Mexico ever since he retired."

"Any relatives?"

"I believe there is one child by an early marriage, and two by another. I don't know where they live, nor do I remember their names." He stood up, walked behind the bar, placed a cup beneath a spout, and pressed a button. It was difficult to imagine Thurman in a beard and long hair. "I handled business affairs for him," he said. "There was a lawyer named Beldon who did his personal work." Coffee suddenly poured out of the spout and then automatically stopped when the cup was full. "I think Beldon died three or four years ago, but his firm still exists, and they should have some records."

"What was he going to see you about?"

Sam shook his head. "If I did know, I couldn't tell you, Gus. But I can tell you that I really don't know. What can you tell me?"

Corona shrugged. "The victim was on the floorboards of an old junky VW bus with an expired registration. It was parked by the seawall at the Yacht Basin. A piece of the victim's shawl, or sarape, or whatever the hell it was, had been cut away. He hadn't been robbed, and apparently it happened around midnight. An anonymous kid called in to report a shooting."

Sam sipped his coffee. Part of his attention was directed toward what Corona was saying, and another part was bringing back from memory what he knew about Cyrus Thurman. They had been

acquaintances more than close friends, although they had met occasionally in the steam room at the Press Club. Cy Thurman had
owned a large amount of stock in a nonscheduled air carrier that he
had started after World War II, and then he had sold out his interests
to a conglomerate for a profit of about two million. Then he had
moved to Mexico. "About two weeks ago I received a letter from
Thurman saying that he had noticed something of a personal nature
which needed to be straightened out," he said aloud. "He said it was
no big deal, but that he would be in my office at eleven on the elev-
enth. That's tomorrow." Again he glanced at the clock on the wall.
"Or today, rather. I don't know what he had on his mind."

"We may have a break this time," Corona said. "A car
burned rubber pretty close to the VW. It went right out over the
curb, and down the street a little way a car was sideswiped. We
don't know if there is a connection, but we're hoping there is. We
may come up with a witness."

Sam glanced toward the opaque sliding doors leading out to
the patio. "In this fog?" he asked.

"That's what Burton said," Corona replied with a shrug.
"You know as well as I do that a tiny detail often breaks a case."

"Why did you come to see me?"

"The press will be after you in the morning because you're
linked. I came over as a favor." He finished his drink. "I'd like to ask
a favor in return."

"Of course."

"Will you come down and see if you can identify the body?
You know how it is. A dead millionaire attracts a lot more attention
than, say, a dead cop." He put his empty glass on a table beside his
chair. "Any time in the morning would be okay."

Sam stood up and carried his coffee cup back to the bar. "I'll
do it right now," he said. "Give me a couple of minutes to get
dressed."

The thought occurred to him, when he was tying his tie, that the detective had more on his mind than the identification of Cyrus Thurman. One of Thurman's children would certainly appear shortly after the morning newspaper was on the street, and it was the usual procedure to have a relative make the identification.

3

---

*T*HE BODY was lying naked on a slab in the morgue. The top of the skull was smashed, but there was so little damage to the face that Sam Benedict had no trouble in identifying Cyrus Thurman, despite the salt-and-pepper beard. The attendant was very professional. One bullet had struck the deceased at an angle high above the bridge of the nose and exited through the right side slightly above. Another bullet had entered high on the back of the head and exited through the top. Either one probably would have been fatal.

"Looks like he had kept himself in good shape," Corona said as the attendant drew up the sheet.

"I remember he used to swim a lot," Sam said, turning away. "I think he was a pilot in the Navy. They might have fingerprints if you want verification."

Corona nodded. "We'll check that out as routine."

"Coffee?"

"Why not?"

The fog was fading when they went out into the street, and the pinkish haze of dawn peeked over the tops of the buildings in the city. The detective held the door open to the all-night coffee stand across from the morgue, and with his other hand he rubbed his fingers along his cheek. "I wish I knew what that 'no big deal' he had for you was," he said.

"What difference does it make?" Sam asked as he slid onto a stool with a dirty red plastic cover.

"Like I said, Sam, it's the little things that are important."

"Now you're talking like a lawyer."

Corona fingered his growing beard. "No," he replied. "A lawyer answers a question by asking another. It's such bad timing. You know something, Sam? It's always bad timing. The relatives always say 'if he only had waited another minute to go to the store, the truck wouldn't have hit him,' 'if she had gone to the beach like she planned, the horse wouldn't have thrown her.' If Cyrus Thurman had only waited one more day to leave Mexico, he wouldn't have been hit by this psycho."

Sam held up two fingers for two cups of coffee. "If he had waited another minute, maybe another truck would have hit him," he replied. "If she had gone to the beach, maybe a riptide would have grabbed her, or a big white shark. Now, what was Cy Thurman doing in a beat-up VW at the Yacht Club? When I knew him, he drove new Cadillacs and wore a gray flannel suit. We don't know who the VW belonged to, and we don't know who killed him."

Corona agreed. "And you don't know who you are defending yet, but you're already defending someone."

24

Sam liked this cop. "I'll dig out the file on Thurman," he said. "If there is anything in there that will help you and won't screw me up with the Canon of Ethics, I'll let you have it."

A radio was playing on the back counter, and the music faded to make way for the six-A.M. news headlines. The first one announced that the Astro killer had struck again.

"Now you know who killed him," Corona said. "The radio just told you."

The door opened, and Burton came in to sit down on a stool next to Corona. He acknowledged the introduction to Sam with a tired nod, then ordered a cup of coffee. "I talked to the guy who owns the Lincoln," he said in an equally tired voice. "He parked the car there about ten thirty. We found another piece of the car that hit it. It was a part of fender emblem saying C-A-T-A. The boys at the garage say the car was probably a Pontiac Catalina not more than a couple of years old. An APB has gone out, and the garages are being notified."

"Give it to the press?" Sam asked.

"Yeah," Burton said. "We traced the VW registration back. It's all paid for, and it belongs to a guy named Ferguson who's doing ninety days on a misdemeanor pot rap in the county jail. He figured his girl friend had it, and he doesn't know where she lives." He sipped from his coffee. "Maxine. He doesn't even know her last name."

Two more men entered. They were strangers, and the thought occurred to Sam that the city was waking up. As if to welcome the new day, the two detectives changed the subject to the Giants.

The night guard in the lobby was still on duty when Sam Benedict entered the foyer of his office building. The guard was new and did not recognize the lawyer until he had signed his name on the register. Then he became overly polite and walked with him to the automatic elevator. Sam received the impression that the man would have ridden up to the office with him, had half an invitation been extended.

Crossing the foyer of his offices, he entered the large informal room that was his private office. Trudy had placed two folders on his desk before leaving the preceding day. One was the file on an income-tax case involving a client with a nine-o'clock appointment. The other file was much thicker and pertained to his eleven-A.M. appointment with Cyrus Thurman. Except for Thurman's last letter and the carbon copy of Sam's reply, the most recent entries concerned the sale of Thurman's stock in the air carrier more than five years earlier. Thurman had come out even better than Sam had remembered. After all the taxes had been paid, he had cleared close to three million dollars.

Sam placed his feet on the corner of the desk, leaned back in his chair, and clasped his hands behind his head. In the year that he had been operating, the Astro killer had struck about once a month. He seemed to like lovers' lanes, and his victims had included a cab driver, a prostitute, and a milkman. When he read the papers now, he certainly would be surprised to find he had caught a multimillionaire. The thought again occurred to Sam that there was much more to Corona's visit than a request to identify the body.

A light began to flash on his call director, and he picked up the telephone. It was Doug Kennedy of the *Chronicle*.

"I hear the Astro got one of your clients."

"You've been listening to the radio," Sam said.

"Nope. Straight from unusually reliable sources."

"What else do you hear?"

"That the victim was Cyrus Thurman, who ran a couple of beat-up World War II surplus airplanes into a couple of million bucks and that he had an appointment with you at eleven this morning."

"Your sources appear to be fairly reliable."

"What did he want to see you about?"

"I don't know, Doug, and if I did I couldn't tell you."

"Did you identify the body?"

"Tentatively." He opened his desk and took out a pad of yellow ruled paper. "Seeing as how you have pulled the files on Thurman, is there anything in there on his children?"

"Just one reference to a child named Albert," Kennedy said. "He was turned over to the custody of his mother when Cyrus got a divorce in 1946. Cyrus married a Dorothy Sloane a few weeks later. No reference to whether or not she foaled. She was killed in an auto accident on bloody Bayshore in 1957." The reporter paused, then added, "Yeah, she was the mother of two."

"Any addresses?"

"Not yet. I hear Cyrus went hippie."

Sam Benedict pushed the tablet away. "That's a question of semantics. He retired and went to live in Mexico."

The reporter chuckled softly. "That's like saying a crazy man with money is merely eccentric. I suppose you are shocked over this senseless killing."

"That's a reasonable quote."

"Any idea what he was doing in a hippie's heap in the Marina District?"

Sam leaned back in his chair. "Not the slightest. When was the last time the Astro came to public attention, Doug?"

"About two weeks ago. He got a bar girl from North Beach."

"If you hear anything, will you let me know?"

"Sure. It goes two ways."

"Of course."

Sam replaced the telephone in its cradle. The newspapers had dubbed the psychopath the Astro. Every time he killed, he cut away a piece of his victim's clothing. Scraps of this were sent to the newspapers and occasionally one of the television stations, along with some astrological doggerel by which the killer attempted to justify his slayings. He killed male and female alike, and there never was any overt sexual molestation. On one occasion he had killed in the daytime in Golden Gate Park, and someone had heard the screams. The police had found the body within a quarter of an hour after the screams were reported, but the murderer had escaped. Later, along with the astrological doggerel and a piece of the woman's bra, had come a boastful letter saying an officer had actually interrogated the Astro, asking him if he had seen anything suspicious. The Astro had described the cop, the cop had been located, but he had asked so many persons the same questions he could not recall one from the other.

The Astro never seemed to run away from the scene of the crime. He just vanished quietly. Two of his first victims had been a couple in a lovers' lane, Sam remembered, and the boy had lived long enough to remember that a "vague shape" had simply opened the back door of the car and started shooting. The "burned rubber" on the pavement that Corona had mentioned must have come from a driver who had seen something. But what could anyone have seen? The fog had been so thick last night that an eyewitness would have had to have been damn near inside the Volkswagen to see anything.

The door opened, and Trudy Black came in carrying two cups of coffee. She wore a blue knit dress with a chain belt around her waist. She was in her early thirties, a good ten years younger than Sam, and last January 2 had marked the first decade she had served as his private secretary. Her black-rimmed glasses were pushed up into her hair, and the thought occurred to Sam that her pert moon face was even prettier when she did not wear her glasses. "What are you doing here at this time of day?" he asked gruffly.

"I'm not a hostile witness on the stand," Trudy replied, placing the coffee in front of him. "So you can remove the cold glare from those deep blue eyes." She sat down in a chair, crossed two well-formed legs, and balanced the cup in her lap. "I have a radio. I listen to the news. I called you at home. No answer. I called here. No answer. Knowing you as well as I do, I presumed that you were en route. I also presumed that I could talk you into buying me breakfast, because I came away without it." She sipped from her coffeecup. "Are you preparing a defense for the Astro?" she asked with a grin.

Sam smiled. "There might be a conflict of interest," he said, and then picked up the telephone as the light flashed. This time it was Bill Montgomery of the *Examiner*. The conversation did not vary appreciably from the one he had with Doug Kennedy.

"Pretty soon the TV will be calling, and then the perimeter papers," Trudy said after Sam had hung up. "If we don't go now, there won't be time for that breakfast you promised me." She stood up and came across to the desk. The telephone light flashed, and she picked up the receiver. "I'm sorry," she said crisply. "He won't be in for at least another hour. May I have him call?" She replaced the receiver as Sam stood up. "Mr. Roger Murphy of the Los Angeles *Times*," she added.

Sam got up from his chair. "If we were married, you would be insufferable," he said with an affectionate smile.

Trudy grinned back. "I accept your proposal, even though it is an improbable time for such a motion to be filed." She picked up the empty cups and walked with him toward the door.

The clock radio turned on at seven thirty. Raquel woke like a large cat, arching her back in the bed and stretching her limbs to the limit. Then she gracefully rose from the bed and stretched again. A moment later she headed for the kitchen to start the water for the coffee. She stopped when she saw Junior curled up on the sofa in the living room, his two bare feet sticking out over the end. She went back to her bedroom to put on a robe. Junior never paid any attention to her running around the house nude, but Father was in some ways still a stranger.

While she was drawing the water, she looked out of the window over the kitchen sink and saw that Junior's VW bus was gone. Her first thought was one of sympathy that her father had been forced to remain overnight with Albert and Althea, and this was followed quickly by another thought that there had been no need for her to go back for a robe.

She remained in the kitchen until the coffee was brewed, then poured herself a cup and walked back into the living room, where she paused, studying her sleeping brother. He wore a pair of pants only. His hands were folded over his breast. It was a feminine gesture, and she wondered again if he was a homosexual. She had never known of him dating a girl. He was almost too gentle for a man. So many of his gestures were effeminate, such as the way he pulled his long hair back over his ears with his fingers. On the other hand, she had never known him to act abnormally around his friends.

Sipping from her coffeecup, she walked out to the front entrance and picked up a copy of the *Chronicle* from the porch, then returned to the living room, placed her coffee on a small table, sat down in an easy chair next to it, and slid the rolled paper out of its string. The headline was very large: ASTRO STRIKES AGAIN.

Directly below the headline was a three-column picture of Junior's car, and for a moment she stared at it uncomprehendingly. The door on the driver's side was open. A black unrecognizable blob was on the floorboards, and a man wearing a topcoat and felt hat was pointing at it with a flashlight. Then slowly she read the story. It was very brief, saying little more than the headline, except that the latest victim was unidentified and the Volkswagen was believed to be the property of a man presently serving a ninety-day term in the county jail. An unconfirmed report stated that in fleeing the Astro had sideswiped a parked car and that police were running down leads from this accident.

She was a strong woman. She wanted to bend her head and cry, but she could not. Not yet. She studied the picture once again. There could not be two such cars in the entire world, and it was parked less than a block from Albert's house in the Marina. She dropped the paper, stood up, followed the long cord of the telephone over to another chair, started to dial, paused as Junior stirred, and carried the telephone into her bedroom. She could not remember Albert's number, and she had to get it from Information.

Althea answered. "Of course not," she said. "It's almost eight, and Albert is always at the Presidio before eight."

"Did you read the paper?"

"I think I have told you that we do not subscribe to either of the local papers. We feel quite strongly about . . ."

"Did Father arrive at your house last night?" Raquel interrupted.

"I think you know he did not," Althea said stiffly. "He had an appointment with Albert at a very unreasonable hour. I went to bed. Albert waited until after midnight; then, knowing that he was at your house and had probably forgotten all about it, he went—"

"Father left here to go to your house," Raquel said angrily. "He was murdered less than a block from your house." She banged down the receiver and realized she had been screaming. For a long moment she sat on the edge of the bed, biting her lower lip to keep the anger within her. Then she looked up and saw Junior standing in the doorway. He was crying, and he made no attempt to stop his tears. He held the paper in his hand.

The tears were infectious, and Junior became almost paternal as he sat down on the edge of the bed and held her to him protectively. For a long time they held on to each other, and then the telephone rang. Raquel answered. It was Albert. "I have already talked to the police briefly," he said in the brusque military tone that he used toward those he considered his inferiors. "Do you have any idea what he was doing in that hippie costume?"

"Oh, Albert," she said. "Not now."

"Just hold yourself together, Raquel. The police are going to be asking me these questions. I want to know where he got that hippie car, and why he came to San Francisco. Do you know why he came up here?"

She hung up on him. The call had had a therapeutic effect in that it brought the anger back and stopped the tears. She looked steadily toward her younger brother, who still sat on the edge of the bed, his hands now clasped loosely between his knees. "Where did you get that car, Junior?"

"I borrowed it." Tears were still in his eyes, but he looked up at her curiously.

"Who did you borrow it from?"

"I didn't borrow it from anyone. It's just one of the heaps around the Art Barn."

"Who owns it?"

Junior shrugged. "How the hell do I know who owns it?"

"You stole it?"

The boy shook his head. "You don't understand. I had to go out to the airport to pick up Dad, so I just went down to the Art Barn and borrowed it."

"Where did you get the keys?"

"The keys were in it."

"So you just got in the car, turned on the key, and drove it off?"

"Yeah. But you don't understand. It's okay."

Once again the tears swelled in her eyes. Junior was so god-damn weak. He gave away everything he owned, and then when he needed something, he borrowed it. "Okay, you just borrowed it," she said aloud. "And then you loaned it to your father, and he was murdered in it. Don't you realize this is a mess, Junior?"

He tilted his head and stared at her.

Raquel nodded vigorously. "And not only a mess, Junior. Trouble. The way the police will look at it, you loaned a car you had stolen to your father, and then he was murdered in it."

Slowly he shook his head. "You don't understand, Quel." He

rubbed the ends of his fingers along his cheeks to wipe away the wet-
ness. "And I'm not a Junior anymore."

"Well, you're sure going to act like one for a little longer,"
Raquel said, suddenly angry. She jumped to her feet and walked
toward the bathroom, peeling off her bathrobe. "Go get the directory
and look up the number for Sam Benedict."

In less than a quarter-hour she had showered, dressed, and put
on a new face. She went out to the kitchen and poured herself another cup of coffee. "What's the number?" she asked Junior.

"I wrote it on the pad by the telephone."

The female voice that answered the call was crisp and
efficient.

"My father had an appointment with Mr. Benedict sometime
this morning," she said. "His name was Cyrus Thurman. My name
is Raquel Thurman." She made her voice equally crisp and efficient.
"Unfortunately, my father will be unable to keep his appointment,
but I shall take the time for myself."

The secretary went off the line for a few seconds, then returned and told Raquel that eleven o'clock had been reserved for her.

She went back to the kitchen, made a large breakfast for both
of them, insisting that Junior eat his portion of the meal. She also was
very firm with her brother just before she left the hillside house.
"First, do not leave here," she said. "Secondly, do not answer the telephone, and thirdly, don't let any strangers in."

"Why?"

"Just one reason, Junior. We don't want to be saying anything to the press until Mr. Benedict tells us what to say."

Junior nodded and went back into the living room. As she
went out the door, she saw him lying down once again on the couch.
She paused, wondering whether or not she should take him with her,
then decided against it.

4

A MESSENGER brought the ballistics report into Corona's small gun-metal-gray office. The detective studied it briefly and then, with a sigh, added it to other documents in a stapled manila folder. For a few minutes he stared at a calendar on the wall; then he picked up the folder and drifted down the long corridor to the office of a deputy chief. The chief's secretary spoke into an intercom. "Gus Corona's here."

"It doesn't look like the Astro," Corona said a few minutes later, sitting down on a sofa across from the chief.

"I wish you'd tell the papers that."

Corona shook his head. "I'd recommend that we wait a little bit," he replied.

The chief shrugged. "What do we have?"

Corona opened the folder. "All of the other killings have been done with the same thirty-two-caliber revolver. This victim was killed by a thirty-eight revolver. More important, there was a new moon last night."

The chief stared at him for a moment, then pursed his lips. "There was a new *what?*" he asked.

"Moon," Corona replied evenly, looking past the chief and out of the window. "Every other time the Astro has moved there has been a full moon in violent aspect to Mars. Mars is a symbol of war and murder."

The chief was silent for a moment, and then sighed deeply. He placed both hands flat on the desk and slowly began to drum the highly polished surface with his fingers. "You believe this crap?" he finally asked.

"No, sir." Corona shrugged. "But the Astro does."

The chief exhaled slowly, then grinned. "You can become the department astrologist," he said, tipping back in his chair. "What else?"

"Thurman left Puerto Vallarta yesterday morning on a CMA plane for Los Angeles. He connected to a United Air Lines flight that arrived here an hour later. He called one of his sons, a Colonel Albert Thurman, from Los Angeles, and the Colonel sent a car out to the airport to meet him. The victim was paged, but did not answer. A United Air Lines ticket agent remembers a man answering the victim's description leaving the flight. One of the women working the magazine rack at the airport reports a middle-aged hippie was reading the papers and that he was met by a young hippie. The description matches."

The detective turned over a paper in his file. "On the VW, it's free and clear and belongs to a Jimmy Ferguson who has served about two months of a ninety-day sentence on a misdemeanor pot conviction. Ferguson says he loaned it to a girl friend. We found her. She loaned to another boyfriend, who drove it down to Big Sur. She

35

says she knows he came back, because she saw him about a week ago, but she didn't think to ask him about the car.

"According to the Colonel, he has a younger stepbrother who is shiftless and a hippie. We've been unable to locate him. The victim also had a daughter, who lives in Sausalito. There is no answer to her telephone. We're checking every half-hour."

"Damn hippies got no sense of property," the chief said. "They're just like those Technocrats that used to be around."

"A blue Pontiac Catalina sideswiped a new Lincoln Continental near the scene at the time of the killing," Corona continued. "About one hundred yards north of the VW were some tire tracks. Rubber was left on the pavement, over the curb, and on the street. The guy was burning rubber as he moved away. It may be the same car that hit the Lincoln."

"What else?"

"Routine. No robbery. A piece of Thurman's sarape was scissored out, and I imagine one of the papers will be getting it soon."

"How did Sam Benedict get into the act?"

"Thurman had a letter from Benedict confirming an appointment. Thurman came up here to see Benedict at eleven this morning."

"Isn't Benedict pretty heavy company for an old hippie to be traveling around with?"

Corona smiled and let the chief have it straight on. "Cyrus Thurman was an eccentric, not a middle-aged hippie. According to Benedict, Cyrus Thurman was worth more than a couple of million clams."

"You don't have to smirk about it," the chief said dourly.

The girl impressed Sam the moment she walked into the office. Her head was held high and her shoulders back. She walked proudly as she came across the room toward him. Her breasts were large, her waist narrow, and she had a woman's hips. Her lips were a little too full, but sensual. Long black hair hung down her back in a pony tail. She sank into a chair in front of his desk, her legs crossing as she moved. Her skirt was high, and she made no attempt to pull it down, but there was nothing coarse in the lack of her not tugging on the hemline. She was all woman, and she was glad of it. He was reminded of an old saying that a lawyer never screws a client, except financially. He smiled pleasantly.

"I want you to represent my brother, Cyrus Thurman, Junior," she said in a slightly demanding tone that might be construed as defensive.

"Why?" Sam asked.

She seemed startled by the short question and looked at him silently before she replied. Then she told him about the Volkswagen bus that Junior had borrowed. She only mentioned lightly the death of her father, presuming accurately that Sam was aware of it, but she did go through the chronology of her father's arrival until his departure for San Francisco.

"Do you know what the Art Barn is?" Sam asked.

"An enclave for would-be artists," she replied. "It's on the North Beach."

"I don't imagine there will be any problem at all about the VW," Sam said. "I'll take care of it."

The girl relaxed. "Why was my father coming to see you?" she asked.

"I don't know. He wrote to me, set the time for the appointment himself, said it was a personal matter, and that it was no big deal."

The girl looked at him searchingly, then nodded and lifted her purse from the floor. She extracted a checkbook and pen. "Is fifty dollars enough for a retainer?" she asked.

Benedict held up his hand. "Do *you* have any idea why your father was coming to see me?" he asked.

The girl shook her head. "If I did, I wouldn't have asked you."

"I handled a lot of business affairs for your father, including the time he cashed in his investments and moved to Mexico," Sam said. "Do you have any idea of how much your father was worth?"

"I have never thought about it. He must have been fairly rich, because he paid Stella a lot of money. He was always sending Junior and me checks."

"Who is Stella?"

"She is his first wife, the mother of Albert. Junior and I are children of his second wife, Dorothy. She was killed in an auto accident."

"If I told you your father was worth approximately three million dollars when he moved to Mexico, would you believe it?"

She laughed and brushed the idea away with the wave of her hand, then suddenly paused. Her eyes widened. "How much did you say?"

"About three million."

Her mouth opened and closed. Either she was a hell of a good actress or she really had no idea of her father's financial affairs. Cy had always been close-mouthed, however. On several occasions he had refused to tell his attorney certain information until he was convinced that it was necessary. "We really will need a lawyer, won't we?" she said after a long pause. "Will you represent us?"

"Who is us?"

"Junior and myself."

"Why not Albert also?"

"I don't feel any responsibility for Albert. I do for Junior."

Sam nodded slowly. "Why don't we leave it this way?" he suggested. "I will represent you. As long as your interests parallel those of your younger brother, there will be no conflict." He nodded toward the checkbook. "Fifty dollars will be fine for a retainer," he said. He watched her closely as she looked at him, and he sensed a furious mental activity behind the quiet dark eyes. After a moment she bent down and scribbled in her checkbook. "I know you were Dad's friend," she said. She slid the corn-colored check across the desk toward him. Her writing was large and bold.

Sam opened the middle drawer of his desk, dropped the check inside, then slowly closed it. He said, "I think it would be very much to your interests to learn why your father made a special trip back to San Francisco to see me."

"Yes?"

"When your father arrived at your home in Sausalito, was he carrying any baggage, such as a suitcase or briefcase?"

"He had a suitcase."

"Is it still in your home?"

"It's in the spare bedroom."

"Then may I suggest that we go to Sausalito and see what might be in it?"

"This is a lot of work for fifty dollars," she said, rising.

Sam nodded. "The retainer is fifty dollars, Miss Thurman. You may consider my total fee to be extraordinarily high, but it will be well within your ability to pay it."

The girl laughed. "I just wanted to see what you would say," she said, letting him hold the door for her as they went into the outer office.

She insisted they ride in her car, a small coupé that looked like a beetle, and was, Sam knew, very expensive and very powerful. And he quickly learned that the girl was not at all shy about using the power she had at her command. They sped up California Street and then down the other side of Nob Hill. When they reached the Golden Gate Bridge, where there was little traffic, the speedometer needle went up to the eighty mark. She shifted down when they turned off the freeway into the narrow road that wound down past the old fort into Sausalito, and Sam sighed, then realized his relief was premature when she whipped down the narrow highway at twice the legal speed limit. "You'll use up your retainer in traffic court," he said when they finally did slow and turn up the hill toward her home. She could not speed here. The road was steep and twisting, but she managed to startle him three times with the cavalier manner with which she cut across the hairpin turns. Then, with a sharp squeal of the tires, she braked and turned onto a platform built out to the road and adjacent to the low-level house, which burrowed into the hillside.

He followed her down the short flight of steps to the entrance and watched appreciatively as she raised a leg to balance her purse while she looked for her key. She threw open the door and went in ahead of him, tossing her purse on a small table and calling out, "Junior?"

There was no answer.

The room was large and tastefully furnished. At one end was a wide French door opening onto a wooden patio. Through it, the city skyline looked like an etching in glass. When he moved farther back into the room, the illusion disappeared, and a corner of Angel Island came into sight. The girl righted a table lamp that had fallen from a small table into a sofa. "Junior?" she called out again. This time he sensed a touch of anger in her cry. There was still no answer. "I particularly asked him to stay here," she said. "He is very unpredictable."

"How would he leave?" Sam asked. "The Volkswagen is impounded."

"He hitchhikes," she said, and then disappeared down a corridor.

Sam walked over to the window. The view was absolutely incredible, and he felt a surge of affection for the area. Below him, going out of the Golden Gate, was a large cruise ship. A few small sailboats bobbed in the bay of Sausalito. From where he stood there was another illusion, one of being suspended in space. The hill fell off so sharply that he appeared to be looking over the edge into the village. There was a portable barbecue stand on the patio. Near a lounge was a towel and some suntan lotion. On a small table next to the lounge was an ashtray with a dead cigar in it. He turned back toward the living room. A pair of very large Hush Puppy boots were lying next to the sofa.

"It's gone," she said curiously, coming back out of the corridor. "I carried it in there myself last night and put it by the bed."

Sam nodded. "That's two things that are gone," he said. "Junior and the suitcase. How did the lamp get knocked over?"

The girl suddenly paled and looked toward the French doors. "The wind sometimes blows it over," she said, her eyes widening as she saw that the doors were closed.

Sam walked over to the door. It was not locked. Taking a handkerchief from his pocket, he pressed against the glass and pushed the door partially open. The wind blowing up from the bay was brisk. He turned and watched the lamp topple slightly, then fall over into the sofa. Sam walked across the small patio and looked down. There was a sheer drop of almost fifty yards; then the hill angled out slightly where it was covered by brush. Lying at the edge of the scrub directly below him was a body. It lay on its back with an arm resting across the eyes, as if to keep out the sun's rays. The stockinged legs were twisted grotesquely inside blue-striped pants. The hair was shoulder length and black. Benedict turned. The girl was standing beside him, looking down. In her hands she held the pair of boots.

5

---

*T*HE COUPLE had been parked
near the San Francisco Yacht Club since shortly after nine in the
morning, and although they sat close together, they did not talk
much or hold hands, or even look at each other, except on occasion.
But from the distance they could have been lovers. They were in fact
detectives attached to the Homicide Division of the San Francisco
Police Department. From where they were parked, they could see
the entire section of the parking lot where the murder of Cyrus
Thurman had occurred the night before.

Earlier in the day, many cars had driven by the murder scene.
Some merely slowed. From others, people had gotten out and walked

around the area. They came out of curiosity, drawn by the same magnet that pulls crowds to the scene of any violent death. In each case, the man in the parked car would relate the license number to the woman, who would note it in the stenographer's shorthand book she held in her lap. Occasionally, if one of the thrill-seekers struck them as suspicious, he would radio the license number into dispatch on a special frequency. Most of the replies that came back within a minute were a laconic "no want, no record." One was a man wanted for several parking violations, but nothing was done, for this operation was not designed to pick up scofflaws.

It was shortly after noon that the first "live" one appeared. The woman snuggled a little closer to her partner the third time the black two-door sedan came past them, moving very slowly, and came to a halt near the tire marks. The detective radioed in the license number, and this time the reply did not come back immediately. There was something that required further checking.

The car backed up slowly, then entered the area, stopping next to the seawall. The door opened to let out a man in his middle forties, with a thin, wiry frame. His cheeks were sunken and his hair a thick bushy white, cut short. He walked slowly to the wall and stared out over the bay, one hand shielding his eyes from the sun. After a few moments, he turned toward the parked police car. The detective put his arms around his partner and kissed her, watching the stranger out of the corners of his eyes. The man stared at them for a long time, then moved away from the seawall and began walking toward them with his head down. When he came to the bloodstains on the pavement, he paused and studied them for a long time. Then, after glancing once again toward the two detectives, he bent down and ran his finger over the stained pavement.

"Raymond Saxeby," the radio said suddenly. "Age forty-eight, 322 Vista Way, Culver City. Two counts aggravated assault, no want."

The man straightened and once again looked over to the necking detectives. Slowly he walked toward them, then paused at the skid marks and studied these carefully. Then he made a 360-degree turn, holding his hands in front of him in a wide V. When he completed his turn, he raised one hand to the angle of a Nazi salute, drew a circle in the air with an extended finger, then bisected it with a swift movement as he dropped his hand. Without a backward look, he turned again, strode to his car, and drove out of the area.

The detective disengaged himself from his companion and picked up the microphone. "That Saxeby one's a loony," he said. "He's heading toward Lombard."

"Okay. We'll watch him," the radio said.

"It's really too much," Raquel said. "It's just really too much. My whole family." She spoke quietly. Gus Corona noticed that the ashtray next to her was overflowing with lipstick-stained cigarette butts. She had not moved from her seat on the soft print sofa since he had arrived more than an hour ago. Then, as if the same thought had occurred to her, she rose abruptly, excused herself, walked into a bedroom, and closed the door.

The Sausalito police had gone. The body had been removed from the hillside with considerable difficulty. The press had come and then departed. There were only three of them left. The detective turned toward Sam Benedict, who sat on a stool at the breakfast bar, both feet firmly planted on the floor, hands clasped behind his head. Corona guessed that the suit the attorney was wearing cost the equivalent of an average cop's three weeks' pay. "No suitcase," the lawyer said. "No matter how many times you ask her, there still is no suitcase of her father's in this house."

Corona sighed. "And the railing on the patio is loose, which means that the boy could have been slammed into it when he went over. Or it could have been loose for some time."

"And she doesn't know, Gus," the attorney said. "She used

the patio for sunbathing and for barbecuing steaks. She hasn't looked at the railing for two years, ever since she moved in here."

"A cop just keeps asking questions, Sam."

"And so do lawyers."

"How did she find you so quick?"

"I'm fairly well known, and her father was a client of mine."

Corona shrugged. "Maybe the autopsy will give us something," he said, "although it's a hell of a long drop down there. If he was as close to his father as she says he was, he could have been despondent."

"But where's the suitcase?" Sam Benedict asked.

The bedroom door opened, and the girl came out. She had changed into tight bell-bottom slacks and a sweatshirt, and she was barefoot. It was the costume for Sausalito. A town full of kooks and hippies, yet this girl apparently was neither.

"You don't think it would be a good idea to stay with your brother?" Sam Benedict asked.

The girl sat down on the sofa again, shook her head, then stood up and carried the full ashtray out to the kitchen. "My brother is dead," she said quietly as she came back into the room. "Albert is my half-brother, and he is insufficiently interested in Junior's death to even call."

"It could be that he hasn't heard," Gus said.

Again the girl shook her head. She sat down on the sofa and brushed the hair back over her temples with her fingers. "He knew five minutes after I told Althea." She lit another cigarette. "I am an intelligent, mature woman," she continued. "I have no suicidal tendencies, and I have been able to take care of myself for years."

Gus Corona silently agreed. There could be some Italian blood in her. She certainly had the full body of a young Italian woman. Her hair was a Sicilian black that matched her eyes. And there was something about her that promised a back scratcher in bed.

45

"We do not dispute that a bit," Sam Benedict said in his low voice. "I think Lieutenant Corona and I are both concerned over your safety."

The girl turned toward Corona, and her eyes looked deeply into his. "You have indicated that three times, Mr. Corona. Why? Do you think someone is engaged in a vendetta to wipe out the entire Thurman family?"

"It is frankly unlikely," Corona said, rubbing the side of his cheek with his fingers. He had been up for more than twelve hours now, and the stubble was thick.

"Did this so-called Astro psychopath kill my father? Did my brother commit suicide, as the local police have suggested?"

The detective shrugged. "I have no answer to either question."

Benedict, sprawled in his seat across from the girl, lit a cigarette and blew out the smoke. "There is nothing to indicate that your father was killed by a psychopath," he said bluntly. "A coincidence is a peculiar happening, and coincidences happen all the time. However, coincidence becomes unbelievable in direct ratio to the number of coincidences that occur during a given time."

Corona sighed as the girl turned her attention toward the lawyer. He studied the curve of her breast underneath the sweatshirt.

"There is a plethora of coincidence here," Sam continued in his best courtroom voice, which Corona knew was demanding the girl's entire attention. "Your father dies shortly before he is to keep an appointment with me. Your brother dies shortly before he is to meet me. Two Thurmans die within twelve hours of each other. Two Thurmans die shortly after leaving you."

The girl stiffened slightly, and her lips tightened.

Sam Benedict paid no attention. "Two Thurmans die violently," Sam said. "And despite the first announced impressions of the Sausalito Police Department, I don't believe your brother committed suicide, nor, I am sure, does Inspector Corona. Why? Where is your father's suitcase?"

He was always a lawyer, Gus thought, always answering a question with another.

The girl slowly turned toward him, and her eyes had widened. "I'm afraid there is no place for me to go," she said, "unless it is to some hotel."

"No close friends?" Sam asked.

"None that are the type I would care to stay with."

Sam sighed. "I have a large apartment on Pacific Heights. I'll have my executive secretary come over as a chaperon, and . . ."

The girl was still looking at him, and Gus Corona interrupted before he realized he was doing so. "If you want to stay here, I'll bodyguard for you." He was suddenly surprised at himself. The chief would be more surprised. The girl was still looking at him, deep into his eyes, and he could read in hers an acceptance and a gratitude that did not need to be spoken. "Maybe I can figure out something tomorrow," she said.

Gus Corona turned toward Sam and noticed that the lawyer was watching him closely. But there was no trace of expression behind his steel-blue eyes. "If you want to send Trudy over here as a chaperon, go ahead," the detective said defensively, and then he relaxed as he saw the lawyer relax. "Why don't you wait here with your client for about two hours while I go check out."

Benedict nodded his agreement. "We do have some private matters we should discuss," he said.

The report of the suicide was on Corona's desk in police headquarters, along with a copy of the evening paper. No one questioned the boy's suicide, but the story was getting banner play because the status of Cyrus Thurman had been discovered. He was described as a multimillionaire eccentric. There was a picture of the boy's body being carried out on a stretcher to a waiting ambulance.

47

Two other pictures identified Lieutenant Colonel Albert Thurman as a Vietnam veteran security officer presently stationed at the Presidio, and Raquel Thurman, a prominent San Francisco interior designer. The youngest son was identified as an artist. Corona put the paper aside for more detailed reading and went through the rest of the reports.

The one on Raymond Saxeby was hot. The suspect had been picked up on Lombard and trailed to a small row house in the Sunset District. He had parked his car outside the garage under the dwelling, walked up the stairs to the main entrance, bent over as if paying a quick obeisance to some shrine, then opened the front door with a key. A check with the utilities companies disclosed that the small house was rented to Saxeby approximately one year earlier. There was no telephone. He was employed as a linotype operator at a job-printing plant on Larkin Street. On this day, he had left the plant before noon, saying that he had the flu. He was taciturn, but when he did talk, the subject invariably was turned toward astrology. His work was satisfactory.

Corona picked up Saxeby's rap sheet, which had arrived from Los Angeles. Three years earlier the suspect had been charged with aggravated assault following a fight with his wife, Marjorie. The charges had been dismissed. The second charge, also aggravated assault, had been filed about eighteen months ago. Again he had beaten up his wife, this time in a tavern parking lot in the Venice area.

Corona drummed his fingers on top of the desk, then picked up the telephone and ordered a two-car twenty-four-hour surveillance of Saxeby. Next he called the Marin County Coroner's office. Cyrus Thurman, Junior, had died of a broken neck. His skull had been fractured, his jaw broken, and two ribs on the right side of the cage were cracked. They were all injuries that could have been caused by the fall. The jaw also could have been broken by a blow that had thrown Junior into the patio railing with sufficient force to loosen it and crack his ribs.

He took an electric razor from his desk drawer and had finished one side of his face before the door opened and Ed Patterson, a reporter for the *Examiner*, came in. "You're screwing up the television set in the press room," the reporter said. "You always start shaving when the news comes on."

"What's going on?"

"Mostly the Astro and the kid's suicide." Patterson gestured toward the open file on Corona's desk. "What is going on at your end?"

Corona continued shaving. "There's been a tentative make on the car that sideswiped that Lincoln," he replied. "It's a late-model blue Pontiac Catalina, and the right-hand side should be stoved in pretty well."

"Want to put it out?"

"Sure, I never keep anything from you guys."

The reporter took some folded copy paper from his pocket and made a couple of notes. "Was young Thurman on a trip?"

"No indication of it. Why?"

Patterson shrugged. "He was a hippie."

Corona shut off the razor and ran his fingers along the side of his face. "He wasn't a hippie. He stood to inherit about a million bucks from his old man, so that makes him an eccentric artist."

"Who gets it now?"

Corona shrugged. "Ask Sam Benedict," he replied.

The reporter laughed and left the room. For a long moment Gus Corona stared thoughtfully at the closed door. The reporter, he decided presently, had asked a very interesting question.

It was a little after six P.M. when Sam Benedict entered his penthouse apartment, poured himself a Scotch, then checked with what he thought was his answering service. But he found that his office switchboard had been plugged through, and Trudy answered his direct line. "How come?" he asked curiously.

"In view of your clients and your propensity for moving them about, I thought you might like me to spend the night in your apartment," she replied.

Sam smiled. "I tried, but a young, good-looking detective beat me out."

"I'm surprised," Trudy chuckled sympathetically. "I called Beldon's office. They have no copy of Cyrus Thurman's will, but there is a notation in the file that Beldon charged him five hundred dollars to draw one up," Trudy continued. "His files were rather poorly organized toward the end. They suggested we talk to Colonel Albert Thurman. His wife is Althea Beldon, who is either the granddaughter or great-granddaughter of David Beldon. They think she may have been given a copy of the will."

"We'll give it a try in the morning." Sam sipped on his Scotch and looked out over the bay. The fog was starting to come in again under the Golden Gate Bridge. "Anything else?"

"Yes. Colonel Thurman called and wants you to call him when you can." She gave him a number, which Sam memorized. He thanked Trudy and hung up.

He finished his Scotch and called the Colonel.

"Oh, yes, Benedict," Colonel Thurman said in a patronizing tone. "Nice of you to return my call. I'd like to have you come out to the house tomorrow about nine."

"Excuse me a moment," Sam replied quietly. He placed the telephone on the table, went over to the bar, where he mixed himself another Scotch and water. He moved slowly, and a good three or four minutes had passed before he picked up the telephone again. "Why?" he asked.

The Colonel had caught the message, and his voice was less patronizing, but still brusque. "You were a friend of my late father, and he was a client of yours. I believe I would like to have you represent me in clearing up his estate. You do have a certain familiarity with his financial matters."

"Yes, I am familiar with some of his financial transactions."

"Do you have his will?" the Colonel asked.

Sam paused, and then said, "I am afraid that there might be a conflict of interest if I accepted your invitation, Colonel."

"Conflict?"

"I represent Miss Raquel Thurman. She gave me a retainer this morning."

There was a long pause. "Well, she certainly wasn't overcome by grief, was she?" the Colonel said. And then the connection was abruptly cut off.

Sam remained by the window, swirling the ice in his whiskey glass. He could not see Sausalito. It was hidden behind Belvedere Island. There was an old saying among the Sicilians that whenever they found the right woman, they were hit by a thunderbolt. Corona possibly was not a Sicilian, but he certainly looked as if he had been hit by a thunderbolt when he first saw Raquel Thurman. He had tried to cover it up, but his attempt had only called attention to the situation. The girl possibly could inherit a million and a half, and that put the odds about a million and a half to one for her ever falling in love with a cop. If Gus was lucky, he would get over it quickly. But not too quickly, he hoped. It would be nice for his client to have a close friend in Gus Corona.

Thurman's will was certainly in Puerto Vallarta, and before they could do much of anything regarding the estate, they had to find the will.

Sam smiled and turned away from the window. The tightest union in the world, next to lawyers and doctors, was that of the policemen. The most practical step now was for a quick trip to Puerto Vallarta. He wondered if Corona could take off a few days and accompany Sam and his client on a trip to Mexico.

A sliver of fog flew past the window. Soon it would be all over the city again.

6

---

*D*ANIEL J. ADAMS was a successful bottle salesman. He sold all kinds of bottles, from liquor bottles that were classified as collectors' items to small plastic bottles which contained liquid hair shampoo. His territory ranged from Seattle to San Diego and as far east as Phoenix and Spokane and everything in between. He traveled extensively, and he chose to live in Burlingame, California, which was near the San Francisco airport and geographically the closest he could come to a reasonable central location for his territory.

On this night, as he arrived on a flight from San Diego, he noticed that the fog had settled over San Francisco, but that the skies were crystal clear over Burlingame. According to his schedule, he would be home for three days, and then return to Los Angeles. His sample suitcases had been left in the southern Californian city, as most of his time in San Francisco would be spent on what he termed his paperwork. At least one day would be spent on the golf course, if he had anything to say about it. Maybe he would spend two days, if he could get through the goddamn paperwork.

He was whistling softly as he came off the intrastate commuter airline and walked up the finger to the main lobby. His son, who was to meet him, was late, or else he was waiting out in front. His son was in neither spot. He was waiting at the entrance to the finger and wore a slightly apprehensive look. "Hello, Artie," Daniel Adams said.

"Hi." He took the briefcase from his father's hand and fell into step beside him.

"What's wrong?"

The boy shrugged. "I banged the car up a little bit."

Now it was Adams' turn to shrug. "That's better than getting kicked out of school," he replied. "Why don't you wait until I get home and have had a couple of martinis before you tell me about it. That way my disposition will be better."

The boy smiled and ran his fingers through his hair. "Sure thing, Dad. Yeah, sure thing."

Still whistling, Daniel Adams crossed the foyer of the central terminal with his son. He was not upset. When he had been a boy, he had banged up a few cars. Banging up a car was just one of the penalties that went with being a father. He would pay one hundred bucks. The insurance company would pay the rest. "How's your mother?"

"She's okay, I guess."

They walked across the street to the parking lot. As they walked down the long row of cars, they were forced to step aside for a black-and-white patrol car of the San Mateo Sheriff's Department. It was moving through the garage with its red light flashing. A moment later a plain black car with a wand of authority jutting from its roof came down the aisle. It came to a halt behind the sheriff's car near the end of the row.

Arthur Adams suddenly paused. His father knew that the two police cars had frightened him. The father raised his hand, snapped his fingers, then turned around. "Maybe you'd better tell me over a cup of coffee," he said. Putting his arm through his son's, he walked back toward the terminal.

"Last night I was with Betty Larson down near the Yacht Club," Artie said, and his voice was frightened. "We heard that guy get murdered—the one by the Astro—and I barreled out of there. It was foggy, and I couldn't see, and I sideswiped this car. It was sort of a hit and run."

Daniel Adams sighed deeply. "If you stayed, you might have been shot?"

"Yeah, I guess."

They crossed the street and went back into the terminal, then took a table in the bar. "A Coca-Cola for him and a double martini on the rocks for me," Adams said to the barmaid, then continued conversationally with his son. "It does not appear that we will be getting home in the immediate future, and I'll be goddamned if I will wait for my martini. Go and call your mother and just tell her that I have some business to take care of and that it might be late before we are home. Was anyone hurt in the accident?"

Artie shook his head. "It was a parked car."

Fifteen minutes later, father and son once again walked back to the garage across from the central terminal. The sheriff's car had disappeared, but the plain black one with the small antenna on the roof now had found a parking stall almost directly across from his Pontiac. The side, he reflected as he came up to it, certainly had been banged. Two uniformed men appeared from nowhere as he unlocked the trunk, and for the first time in his life he knew how it felt to have a gun pointed at him by two men who would not hesitate to pull the trigger. He dropped his case and raised his hands. His son followed his movements precisely.

A man with a slight paunch emerged from the plain car, burped, and walked over to them. He ran his hand over both father and son. "Your car?" he asked, moving back. His hand went into a hip pocket and pulled out a worn wallet which he flipped open to expose a badge. "Detective Lars Burton, San Francisco Homicide."

"It's my car. My name is Daniel Adams."

"May I see your identification?"

Daniel Adams slowly extracted his wallet from a jacket pocket and took out his driver's license. At the same time, he purposely let the detective see his sleeves of credit cards.

Burton examined the license carefully, comparing the picture, then passed it back and motioned for the two detectives to put away their guns. Then he nodded toward the car. "How'd it happen?" he asked mildly.

"My son was necking in the Marina last night when he heard gunshots that apparently killed that man," Adams replied. "Rather than get shot at, he decided to run away. He sideswiped a parked car in the fog."

The detective sighed deeply. "That figures," he said tiredly. "It was too easy. Do you mind coming downtown for a statement?"

"Right now?"

Burton looked at his watch. "It's late, and you probably want to get home," he said. He turned to the boy. "What did you see?"

"I didn't see anything except for some headlights when this VW came up. Then I heard this guy walking with metal cleats on his heels. Then a little while later we heard the shots. After that, we heard the woman scream."

"A scream?"

"Yeah. It was after I creamed the car."

"How do you know it was a woman?"

"You know. It sounded like a woman."

"Where?"

The boy shook his head. "It was in back of us somewhere, I guess."

Again the detective sighed. He turned to the father. "Maybe we'd better get a preliminary statement inside. We can probably borrow some office space."

"Of course. If my son is going to be in difficulty because he left the scene of an accident, however, maybe I should get a lawyer."

"I'm not going to cite him, but you can get a lawyer if you want. We're not trying to make a case against your boy. We're just looking for help."

Daniel Adams shook his head. "Let's go find an office," he said. "Leaving the scene is better than getting shot."

"I'll buy that," Burton replied. "It's a hell of a lot better than getting shot."

Gus Corona sat in the chair with his coat off and his tie loosened, but he still felt uncomfortable. The gun in the holster fastened to his belt seemed ostentatious, but then, it would appear more ostentatious if he made a point of taking it off. The girl was quiet, but occasionally she would get up from her chair and pace around the room. She wore sandals, bell-bottom slacks, and a jersey sweater. Her hair now was loose and hung down over her shoulders, and every once in a while, when she walked, she would shake her head and brush her hair back over her shoulders. Once she asked if he wanted a drink, and when he said coffee only, she went into the small kitchen and made a Silex pot of coffee. Since then, he had downed three cups, and she had had two Scotches. Now she made herself another, and as she went out to the kitchen to splash some water in the glass, he wondered if she planned to get drunk.

"How did you get out here?" she asked from the kitchen. She was standing by the sink, looking out of the window.

"I drove."

"I think your car is gone."

"I left it down the street. It's a white Volvo."

"Oh." She came back into the room and sat down across from him. She had a peculiar way of sitting down, crossing her legs before her fanny hit the chair. "Is that your own car?"

He nodded. "I'm a San Francisco cop," he said. "This is Sausalito."

"You mean you're not getting paid to nursemaid me?"

"It would be a criminal act to take money for such an assignment." He smiled.

She did not smile back. "If you're not getting paid, then why don't you take off that silly gun and your shoes and have a Scotch. I'm afraid I don't share either your or Mr. Benedict's fears that I might be in jeopardy."

He unbuckled his wide belt and slid the holster and gun off, then placed it on the table beside him. "Make it weak," he said, with a tentative grin. "As long as I'm here, I don't think you are in any jeopardy."

"Why don't you help yourself?" She nodded toward the bar.

He made no move to rise, pushing her a little, and she had just started to get up when the telephone rang. She answered it with a crisp "yes" and sank back into the chair. He listened to her side of the conversation.

"I doubt it very much. There would be no point to it. . . . He never mentioned it, but I imagine there is. . . . Probably in Mexico. . . . Junior is at the Sausalito Mortuary. Father is at Emerald Green. . . ." She pushed the telephone away for a quick gulp at her drink. "Before the funerals?" She paused. "I guess there is no reason why not, if you think it is important. . . . Yes, he's here." She held the telephone toward him. "It's Sam Benedict," she said, and rose and walked over to the bar.

The attorney was in one of his persuasive moods. His voice was unctuous, but with the same persistent, demanding tone that Gus

Corona sometimes had seen him use in court. "I need someone who is influential in police circles in Mexico, Gus. Who do you know that would be willing to meet us in Puerto Vallarta tomorrow?"

Corona nodded. "I have a friend who is a captain in the Mexican secret police. His name is Eduardo Campeche. What do you mean, 'meet us' in Puerto Vallarta?"

"I happened to be talking to the chief, and he tells me you have seventy-four hours in overtime, and the thought occurred that you might like to do a little moonlighting. We leave here at nine and catch a ten-thirty flight out of Los Angeles. We shouldn't have to stay more than a day."

Raquel came to his side and passed him his drink. "What's my role, Sam?"

"I may need an impartial witness." The lawyer hesitated, then added, "Just meet me at the United boarding gate for the commuter flight tomorrow morning at eight thirty." He hung up.

Shaking his head slowly, Gus Corona replaced the telephone in its cradle. Sam Benedict had been working late, because at this time of night it would take a deputy chief, at least, to find out how much time off one Lieutenant Gus Corona had accrued. He called headquarters and was not in the least surprised to learn that he had already been marked down as taking the next three days off. In addition to having influence, Sam Benedict was blessed with a remarkable sense of confidence in his ability to persuade a person to do his bidding.

"Are you hungry?" Raquel asked. "I can make something."

"Okay." He sipped his drink and watched her as she went out to the kitchen. She wore no bra. That was very good.

"What time did he say we were to meet him?" she asked from the kitchen.

He stifled a quick surge of pleasure over the knowledge that she also was coming. "We meet him at eight thirty," he replied evenly. "Did he tell you why he was in such a hurry?"

She came to the kitchen doorway holding a fistful of hard spaghetti. "He didn't say why the hurry. He just said we should gather up any papers Daddy might have left down there."

Gus nodded. Before anyone else does, he thought. And Sam Benedict was looking for a little protection just as much as he was for an impartial witness. He smiled slightly. "I'm going to have to call Mexico City," he said.

She waved toward the telephone and turned back toward the stove. As he reached for the instrument, however, it rang, startling him, and he realized that he was uptight.

"Answer it, will you, please," she called.

He picked up the telephone. "Miss Thurman's residence."

There was no answer other than the sound of heavy breathing from the receiver for about four or five seconds before the connection was broken.

"Who was it?" Once again she was back in the doorway.

He shrugged. "They hung up. They didn't say. Probably your boyfriend."

"There's no one I know who would be upset if a man's voice answered my phone," she replied, spacing her words evenly.

"You get many crank calls?"

"Never have yet." She turned back to the kitchen, tore a paper towel from a roll over the counter, and dried her hands. "You don't think it was the Astro who killed my father, do you? None of you think that, do you?"

"We don't know. There are certain signs which indicate that it was. There are other signs to indicate that it wasn't."

"What indications are there against it being the Astro?"

He shrugged. "Someone came out and took your father's suitcase. Your brother died, and you say he was not the type to commit suicide." He watched her from the kitchen doorway as she broke the spaghetti into short lengths so it would fit into the pot of boiling water. She probably wasn't Italian. No Italian would do that. "Then there is the matter of the moon," he continued aloud. "Every other time the Astro has gone berserk, it has been on the night of a full moon."

"When it was in violent aspect to Mars," she added.

"I was just going to say that."

She reached up into a closet, the movement separating the bottom of her sweater from the top of her pants. She was tanned, and the stomach was flat. The can she took out was labeled "meatballs in tomato sauce," and he knew there was no way she could be Italian. "You're a Taurus," she said, sliding the can under an electric opener.

"You're only working against twelve-to-one odds," he said. "You're bound to hit it once in a while."

"I really don't believe in it."

"On the other hand, there are more domestic fights on the night of a full moon than any other night of the month. And it seems to have affected the Astro."

"You were going to call Mexico City," she replied.

He had forgotten about it. He could handle liquor, and he could handle tobacco, but an attractive woman could make him as irresponsible as a drunk. It took him about a half-hour to run down his friend, Captain Eduardo Campeche. The Mexican detective was in Tijuana and he would be unable to get away until about noon, as he was required to testify in a court case.

Gus Corona relayed this news to Sam Benedict, and the attorney quickly came up with an alternative suggestion. They would fly to Burbank in the morning, where a chartered plane would be waiting for them. They would then proceed to Tijuana, where Campeche would have customs clearance, and then on down to Puerto Vallarta. The detective placed another call to Tijuana. Campeche was agreeable.

"I'll probably have to stay down there," Raquel said a moment later, placing two dishes of spaghetti and meatballs on the small breakfast bar. "I'll owe Mr. Benedict more than my share of the entire estate."

They ate silently, and when they had finished, she put the plates in a built-in dishwasher and flicked a cloth around the tiny room a few times, making it appear immaculate. "If we are going to get up at six," she said, "I think I'll try to get some sleep now." She pointed toward the corridor. "You know where the guest room is," she added, and without waiting for an answer, she went through the living room to her own bedroom and shut the door.

The sound of a telephone ringing awakened him, and in the dark it took him a moment to orient himself. Then he remembered that the telephone was one with a long extension cord and that he had left it on the floor next to the sofa. Slowly he rose, slipped on his pants that he had draped over the back of a chair, and stepped toward the corridor. At the doorway he paused as a light came on in the living room. From force of habit, he looked at his watch. It was two thirty exactly. He walked out into the corridor, then paused again and silently caught his breath. She was bending over, naked, her breasts hanging down from her body as she picked up the telephone. As she straightened, she saw him and she nodded drowsily. "Hello," she said. Then suddenly she shook her head. "I beg your pardon?" She placed her hand over the mouthpiece. "Someone wants to know if I am alone," she said.

"Tell him yes." He walked toward her.

"Yes, we are alone," she said into the telephone. "I mean yes, I am alone. Hello? Hello?" She took the phone from her ear, looked at it curiously for a second, then replaced it in its cradle. "He hung up," she said, swaying slightly. She was still half-asleep. Placing the telephone on the sofa, she turned and walked back into the bedroom, still swaying as if she were drugged or drunk.

For a long time he remained quietly in the living room, painting a mental picture of her bending over to pick up the telephone.

Mama mia, he thought. She had a body that would make a priest forget his vows. After a while he sighed deeply, wet his lips, turned to go back to his room, then paused as he realized the light was still on in her bedroom. Again he waited motionless for a long time, and then, feeling more like an intruder than a guest, he walked over to the door and looked in. She was lying on her back in the bed with one leg on the floor. Her hair was fanned out over the pillow and one arm was across her eyes to shut out the light from the bedroom lamp. The window was wide open, and a cool breeze came in, pushing the draperies aside and blowing on her body, causing the skin to goose-pimple. Her chest rose and fell evenly, and the large nipples on her breasts had contracted and stood erect.

Again he took a deep breath, moistened his lips, and silently moved over to the bed. There was no empty pillbox on the table, just a glass of water. Her breathing was not labored. Very gently he raised the electric blanket up to her shoulders. As he straightened to turn out the light, she moved under the blanket. The tempo of her breathing changed. He flicked off the light on the bed table, then silently began to move toward the door.

"What do you want?" Her voice was strained, uptight.

He stopped. "You forgot to turn out the light, that's all."

She exhaled in the manner of a child who has been holding his breath for a long time. "I'm scared. Suddenly I'm scared."

"Everything is okay. I just turned out the light."

"Hold me. Please hold me." She was crying. "Please."

He went back to the bed, his heart pounding.

For a long time he lay beside her, on top of the blanket, arms around her; she cried quietly, her face nuzzled in his neck, her tears spilling down over his chest. After a while her breathing once again became paced to sleep, but when he tried to pull his arm from beneath her, she woke, rolled over on her back, and placed her hand on his chest.

"You're cold."

"I'm all right."

"Did I cry out?"

"I don't follow you."

"I had a nightmare. I dreamed I went out to answer the telephone, and there was a man there with a gun."

Again he wet his lips, acutely aware of the continued painful throbbing in his groin. "The phone did ring, and I was in the living room when you answered it."

She was silent for a moment. "Who was it?" she asked.

"A crank. There are a lot of sick people who get their kicks on a telephone."

"Oh." She sat up, and the blanket fell away from her breasts. He sensed, more than he could see, that she stared at him in the dark. Her hand dropped between his legs, felt his need, then raised and tugged at the snaps on the waistband of his pants.

A moment later she drew her knees up to her shoulders and guided him into her. "Oh, God," she moaned. Gus Corona suddenly felt he was very much of a man, and he knew that he was not the object of charity.

7

ALTHOUGH THE COMMUTER flights
sat six abreast, Sam Benedict was unable to get three seats together. It
was always a hassle to get on board one of these flights, as those on
first got the seat preference. The flight was in its final boarding proc-
ess when Gus Corona and Raquel Thurman came running up to the
check-in gate, and the only seats left on the plane were a few isolated
middle seats far apart. Corona appeared tired, but the girl appeared
fresh. Both traveled light, however, which would be a help.

After the flight was airborne, Corona came over to Benedict
and said that there had been a couple of interesting developments, but
nothing that could not wait until they got to Los Angeles, then re-

turned to his seat. Sam tried to settle back in the too narrow slot to read the paper. There was nothing that interested him particularly, at least on the first page. He could not turn the pages without elbowing the passengers on both sides of him. He finally sighed and for the next forty-five minutes sat with the paper in his lap.

The twin-jet Aero Commander was waiting for them a few yards from the gate where the commuter flight pulled in at the Hollywood-Burbank airport. The two pilots wore business suits, were very informal, but very efficient. One of them managed to acquire the proper bags from the ground crew before they were sent out to the baggage-receiving area. There were only two, one each for the detective and the girl. Sam carried everything that he needed in a combination briefcase that fit under the seat of the airplane.

"Do you have your tourist permits?" one of the nonuniformed pilots asked.

"Arrangements have been made to pick them up in Tijuana," Sam replied, looking toward the detective, who nodded agreement.

The small executive jet was as comfortable as the commuter jet had been uncomfortable. Its takeoff was much more dramatic because of the rate of climb, although Sam knew that the overall speed was somewhat slower than a commercial jet's. It would be nice to own one, but then, one and a half million was a lot of money for a toy.

"I'm getting a lot of service for my fifty-dollar retainer," the girl said.

Sam smiled. "I told you it wasn't the retainer that would be high," he replied.

She shrugged and looked out of the window. Her skirt was split up the front, and she wore boots that came almost up to her knees. The dress was made of leather. He noticed that she wore no jewelry and that her lipstick was so pale as to be almost unnoticeable.

"I talked to Lars Burton this morning," Corona said. "The

hit-run and the tire skids were made by a kid who was parked at the seawall with his girl. The kid heard two spaced shots, a character walking fast with metal cleats in his heels, and after he sideswiped the car, he heard a woman scream."

Sam assumed a thoughtful look.

Gus Corona shook his head. "If the elder Thurman had picked up some woman, he did it only a few minutes before he was killed. The toll taker at the Golden Gate Bridge remembers him going through alone. He made the trip from Sausalito in about forty-five minutes, even in the fog."

Raquel looked toward him. "How do you know the time so well?"

"He left your house at eleven. The kid noticed the time after he had sideswiped the car, and it was eleven fifty-five. He remembers it because he had to go all the way to Burlingame, and he was supposed to be home by midnight."

"Has anyone talked to Colonel Thurman and his wife?" Sam asked.

"One of the detectives took a statement. They waited until about midnight, then assumed that the elder Thurman had decided not to come. They didn't hear a thing."

"I think it very strange that only two people in that area were able to hear gunfire and screaming," Raquel commented.

Corona nodded. "A lot of people don't see anything either. Someone gets gunned down in a crowd, and you can't find a person who saw a thing."

"Any other developments?"

"Two telephone calls at Raquel's house. I answered the first. It was the heavy-breather type who hang up. She answered the second. It was some guy whispering who wanted to know if she was alone. Odds are that both of them are cranks."

The girl turned toward the detective, looking at him with affection.

"I've arranged for taps and tracers," Corona continued.

The girl reached out and placed her hand on Corona's forearm. It was a gentle touch, and he appeared to ignore it.

"If a woman screamed, there may have been three witnesses," Sam said.

"We're checking missing persons," Gus replied. "But the two kids only heard. The fog was never thicker. It's unlikely that anyone saw anything." He put his hand on top of Raquel's and squeezed it gently, moving it from his arm. She smiled and once again looked out of the window.

"Where was the screaming woman?"

"She just screamed once. Both of the kids say it came from behind them."

The plane banked sharply, and Sam saw the city of San Diego below. The plane began its rapid descent, and a few minutes later its wheels touched down on the runway of the Tijuana International Airport, just across the border. When Sam turned his attention back to the detective, he saw that Corona and the girl were holding hands. The two hands did not unclasp until the plane came to a stop in front of the terminal building.

Gus Corona had done his job well, Sam thought, stepping off the plane. Two Mexican soldiers treated them with the deference accorded a big roller in Las Vegas as they guided them toward the building entrance. Another officer asked them the vital statistics necessary to fill out the forms. Presently a giant wearing a loud checkered sports jacket, bright blue pants, and a white turtleneck sweater strode into the building from the street entrance. He dwarfed everyone in the room. His hands were huge. If clenched in a fist, they could have the crunching force of a sledgehammer, Sam thought, as the man approached them. Then, as Corona straightened up from the desk, the giant beamed and held out his arms. A second later he and Corona were embracing each other in the Latin manner. Eventually Corona broke loose. "El Capitán Eduardo Campeche," he said dramatically, "this is Miss Raquel Thurman and the Mr. Sam Benedict."

Campeche bowed toward the girl, then turned toward Sam. "I'm glad to know you, tiger," he said in a voice that boomed with the enthusiasm of a Los Angeles used-car dealer. A lieutenant, carrying a small suitcase and a garment bag, came out of the inner office and handed them to Campeche. Sam heard him say in Spanish that everything was cleared and that they could depart anytime.

A quarter-hour later they were airborne once again, and fifteen minutes later they were over the waters of the Sea of Cortez. For the first part of the flight, Raquel sat silently looking out of the window while Corona briefed his Mexican counterpart on the events in San Francisco. Campeche appeared to absorb them easily, although he had not heard of the Astro killings, a point which should not be considered odd, he pointed out, as his companions probably had never heard of the Jalisco strangler. But then he took out a long panatela cigar, peeled off the cellophane, and stuck the end of it in his mouth. "Okay, Sam," he said pleasantly. "I have heard a lot about you, and I know you want something more than just having a little grease through customs."

Raquel recrossed her legs, and Sam noticed both of his companions glance at her, and it occurred to him that it might have been wise not to have brought her. "We're primarily looking for a will," he said, "and whatever other pertinent personal papers Mr. Thurman may have left down here."

"Pertinent to what?" Campeche asked.

"To whatever business that he had with me. I feel that this has a bearing upon the future actions of my client." He leaned toward the big Mexican. "With you along, quite probably there will be no objection on the part of his household to our looking through his effects. They might be more willing to talk to me in your presence than they would to someone they don't know from another country."

"I'll go along with that, tiger," Campeche replied. "Within reasonable limits."

Sam looked at him, then grinned. "I particularly want to ensure that nothing is done that can be considered illegal in any manner."

"I understand perfectly," the captain replied.

"Good," Sam replied, and leaning back in his chair, he closed his eyes. Before he fell asleep, he heard Corona explain, "Sam feels that an airplane was made for sleep. If you cannot exercise and if you cannot write or read satisfactorily, then it is foolish not to utilize the time by storing up sleep."

Campeche chuckled softly and asked the girl if she objected to cigar smoke.

The sun was a red ball in the sky when he awoke and straightened the seat back. Both Corona and Raquel were asleep. The Mexican detective had taken a chair up against the bulkhead and was reading a paperback mystery novel. They were low over the ocean, and presently he felt the abrupt slowing in speed and the slight dip of the nose as the flaps were extended. A few minutes later they arrived with the sunset in Puerto Vallarta. Gus and Raquel awoke with the bump of the wheels on the runway.

Campeche folded his book and placed it in his jacket pocket. "Where are you staying?"

"I made reservations at the Oceana," Sam said.

Raquel folded her compact. "There's room at the house," she said casually. "Why don't we all stay there?"

"You have been here?" Sam asked, somewhat startled.

"No," she replied, snapping her purse shut. "But Daddy told me several times that there are nine bedrooms."

"That indeed seems to be an adequate number for six persons," Sam replied.

There was no trouble getting through the customs area. It

had all been taken care of in Tijuana, Campeche explained. There was trouble, however, in getting out of the airport. Because no flights were expected, no taxicabs were around the tiny terminal building. Campeche, however, finally found a guard who, after looking at the giant's badge, took him to a working telephone. About three-quarters of an hour later two decrepit taxicabs pulled up in front of the small terminal building. Both of the drivers knew where Señor Thurman lived.

They rode a short distance on a paved highway, Sam Benedict, Campeche, and one of the pilots in the lead car, but then, as they entered the village, the road became extraordinarily rough, so rough that pedestrians moved faster than the cars. A man wearing a sombrero and a sarape pushed an ice-cream cart down the street ahead of them. The weather was humid, but not unpleasant because of the breeze that came off the ocean. There was the smell of salt water and Mexican cooking oil and fish and flowers. They were pleasant, happy smells, and Sam suddenly understood how a man could decide that this was preferable to the competitive life of the city. Then the big Campeche lit another cigar, and the smell of the tobacco overcame the more subtle odors of the town. The road turned and elbowed its way through the community. At one moment they were driving so close to the ocean that he could see the soft surf washing up on the shore. A moment later they appeared to be miles from the sea, trapped between two rows of narrow buildings. Presently the road straightened and became a smooth gravel, and they began to climb up the side of a mountain, only to dip down again, then climb. After traveling about two miles along this road, the cab pulled up in front of a large house built into the side of a hill. The building was down the hill, and the entrance to it was guarded by a wrought-iron gate. Below the gate was a circular cement patio, and parked here was a Jeep and a late-model sports convertible with Mexican plates, clearly visible in the fading daylight.

One of the cabdrivers blew his horn, and the other immediately echoed him. Someone invisible below called out in Spanish that there was no one at home.

Campeche opened the cab door and went to the gate. *"Poli-cia! Venga aquí!"* he said, his voice rumbling down the incline. "Police! Come here."

A door slammed, and a thin wiry Mexican with graying hair came out of the shadows and walked slowly up the incline. He talked quietly with the Mexican detective for a moment, then stepped back, pushed a button on the inside stanchion, and the gates slowly swung open. Campeche remained with the caretaker by the gate as the cabs went down the short drive to the house and turned around in the short circle. Sam knocked tentatively on the massive carved door, but there was no answer, nor was there any sign of a bell or knocker.

Everyone had forgotten to convert their currency to pesos, and an argument arose with the taxi drivers, until Raquel, speaking sharply in Spanish, convinced each to take an extra United States dollar and change it in the village. The cabs ground up the inclined driveway and passed through the gates, which swung together behind them.

Campeche and the caretaker came down the slope talking earnestly. When they reached the driving turnaround, the caretaker once again disappeared into the shadows. "He has to go down to his own apartment and get a key," Campeche said, dragging on his cigar. "Looks like you may be a little late, tiger."

"Why?"

"A lawyer came out from the town this morning, according to the caretaker. He told the servants that Thurman had been murdered, paid them off, except for the caretaker, then went through the old man's study and went away with some papers."

"How does he know the man was a lawyer?" Sam asked.

Campeche chuckled. "He left a card and a receipt for the papers. We'll find out soon. The receipt and the card are inside the study."

"It's probably Albert," Raquel said indifferently. "He would think of something like this."

The huge carved door opened in front of them, and the caretaker bowed slightly, as if he were a host. The door went well with the room. It was immense, and it was a man's room. The far wall was solid glass, but because it faced the ocean there were no lights, and now it appeared as a solid black mass. The floor was a Spanish red tile, and between the numerous large scatter rugs were jaguar pelts and skins of cougar. The chairs were big and comfortable, as were the sofas. It was the kind of a room, Sam thought, that would make an interior decorator shudder. The caretaker spoke once again, and Campeche nodded. "He's sent a boy for the servants."

"Yes," Raquel said.

The caretaker bowed once again and motioned for them to accompany him. He led them past a long bar, then down a curling flight of stairs. Sam realized that they were in a three- or four-story house with the main entrance on the top floor. The floor below had been designed to curve with the slope of the hillside. The building curved, and each of the bedrooms was shaped in the manner of a piece of pie, with the narrow end at the entrance.

Campeche translated for the caretaker again. "He says to take any room you wish. The *criadas* will be here soon, and a dinner will be ready in about three hours, if that is agreeable." The giant chuckled. "They eat late in Mexico, you know."

Sam smiled. "I would like to see the lawyer's card," he said quietly.

He tossed his small suitcase in the first bedroom as Campeche translated, and Raquel did the same in the next bedroom. As they walked around the curve of the building, the pilots disappeared into their rooms and Corona into the next. At the end of this curving hall was still another winding staircase that ended in a room about three-quarters the size of the one on the top floor. One wall was glass. The others were lined with books from ceiling to floor. In one corner of the room was a large easy chair positioned under a hanging lamp. Near this was a large desk, bare on the top, but for a pen set, which now was used as a paperweight for a piece of legal-sized, lined yellow notepaper and a small business card.

Campeche picked up the paper and read it aloud. "Received from the custody of Antonio Sánchez, estate keeper for the late Cyrus Thurman, photostat copies of one will; three birth-certificate copies, one each for Albert Thurman, Raquel Thurman, and Cyrus Thurman, Jr.; and certain other personal documents, three in number; a title deed to certain property in Puerto Vallarta; and a passbook for the Bank of Mexico. Signed Manuel Castellenano P."

The business card stated that Manuel Castellenano P. was an attorney practicing in Puerto Vallarta, and it listed two telephone numbers, one for his residence and the other for his office.

The Mexican detective turned toward the caretaker and spoke to him rapidly in Spanish, so rapidly that Sam found it difficult to follow him, but he noticed that Sánchez suddenly appeared uneasy. When he replied, he looked down at his feet, and his voice was soft.

"If Señor Castellenano is a lawyer and a man of good reputation, there is nothing wrong in him giving him the papers," Raquel said. "It was not for him to decide."

Campeche shrugged. "I wondered how he knew where the papers were, Señorita."

"And the lawyer found them in the desk," she replied, then turned toward Sánchez and smiled briefly.

"Maybe we can reach Castellenano," Sam suggested, picking up the Ericson-style telephone on the bottom shelf of a table next to the easy chair. The Mexican attorney was at home. He was surprised that there was an adversary situation, and he would be at the Thurman residence in a little moment to discuss the matter.

When he put down the telephone, Sánchez had left the room. Sam looked carefully around the study. If there was a safe, it probably would take a full day to find it. Each one of the books would have to be removed. These were no "Books by the Yard." They all had a well-read look, and Cy's taste certainly had been varied, as the volumes ranged from Dickens to recent best sellers in the United States.

Raquel seemed to read his mind. "About once every two months he would send me a check for one hundred dollars and ask me to send down some more books. He'd read just about everything."

"Do you remember on what banks the checks were drawn?" Sam asked.

"Sometimes Bank of America. Other times Wells Fargo."

Sam made a mental note. "Señor Castellenano is en route," he said. "We can meet him upstairs as well as here."

A "little moment" for Señor Castellenano was approximately an hour. He was a young man, expensively dressed, who radiated efficiency and spoke fluent English. He shook hands like a Rotarian, accepted a straight gold tequila from Raquel, and spoke first to Campeche. "I have heard of you from *Coronel* Ricardo Martínez," he said quietly. The manner in which it was said told Sam that the Mexican attorney was telling Campeche that he had political connections.

"That is very good," Campeche replied lazily. "Then you know that I have a certain amount of authority."

Castellenano nodded. "But I am curious as to why the Mexican secret police have an interest in this unfortunate affair."

Campeche chuckled softly. "It is not important enough to take up your time with explanations, Señor," he replied.

The Mexican attorney shrugged, glanced toward Raquel and smiled, then turned to Sam Benedict. "And I have heard of you, Señor, through your book *Benedict on Blackstone*. I have the feeling that we both are reasonable men. What can I do to help?"

Sam smiled an acknowledgment, placed an ankle on his knee, and sprawled in his chair. "I represent Miss Thurman, who is one of the heirs to this estate and who probably will be named administra-

74

trix. We came down to gather up the necessary papers for probate."

Castellenano raised his eyebrows. "I was under the impression that there was only one heir, a Colonel Albert Thurman of San Francisco."

"No. You have been given a wrong impression."

The Mexican attorney hesitated, glanced toward Raquel, then back to Sam. "Perhaps it would be better if we talked confidentially," he suggested.

Raquel shook her head. "I'm a big girl," she said evenly.

"I presume you are representing Albert Thurman," Sam said.

"Indirectly." Castellenano nodded. He put down his tequila, opened his briefcase, and pulled out a yellow pad of ruled paper. "This morning I received a call from a Mr. Howard Dredge of the firm Beldon and Dredge in San Francisco, California. He told me the tragic news and informed me that he was representing the heir to the estate, a Colonel Albert Thurman. At his request, I came here to see if there was a will, or any other pertinent papers. He asked me to send them to him. He also asked me to look out for the Colonel's interests in the property. I discharged the servants, as you know, located the photocopies of the requested documents, as you know, but was unsuccessful in finding the originals." He dug into his briefcase again and pulled out a sheaf of photostats stapled together. "I have no objection to your looking at them," he added, getting up and passing them to Sam. "I believe the phraseology of the will may be of significance, although I am sure it is contestable."

Sam picked up the sheaf of photostats proffered him. The top one was the first page of a will, and Sam had read no more than the first paragraph before he put them down with a studied carelessness. "What are you planning to do with these?" he asked.

The Mexican attorney shrugged. "It was my understanding that Mr. Dredge represented the executor of the estate," he replied. "It was my plan to send them to him."

Sam frowned. "The administrator has to be determined by

the probate court in San Francisco," he said. "I am not familiar with Mexican probate law, but I should think that these papers should be kept here in the house until there has been a ruling. You see, it is my feeling that Miss Thurman should be named administratrix of the estate."

Again Castellenano shrugged. "These are but copies. It is of little importance. I am informed that the late Señor Thurman carried the originals with him when he went to the United States."

"May I ask who so informed you?"

"The caretaker, Antonio Sánchez. He told me this afternoon that a few days past, Señor Thurman called him into this room and showed him a copy of his will. Sánchez says Mr. Thurman told him that it was a will, explained what a will was, and that he was going to have it rewritten in order that Sánchez would get one hundred thousand pesos when Señor Thurman died. It is possible, of course, that Sánchez is not telling the truth."

"My father would do that," Raquel said quietly.

"Sánchez told me that is why Señor Thurman was going to the United States, in order that he might have the will rewritten. He said also that there was a woman who also was to be left a similar sum."

"And who was that?" Sam asked.

The Mexican lawyer looked toward Raquel, then sighed. "A woman of not good reputation, but one for whom your father had maintained a continuing fondness."

"Good for him," Raquel said.

Sam held up his hand. "I think these photostats should be kept right where they were until there is a court disposition here," he said with a worried frown. "None of us wants to become involved in any irregularity."

"They should never have been removed," Campeche commented, pulling on his long panatela. "I agree with Señor Benedict that they should remain here until the matter has been decided by the court."

Castellenano glanced toward the detective. "I thought I was representing the executor, Capitán," he said easily, "in which case there would have been no problem." He waved his arm. "Restore them to the lower-right-hand drawer of the desk downstairs after you have read them." He stood up and closed his briefcase. "But after you have read them, I think you will agree that Mr. Dredge's client probably will be appointed executor." He bowed slightly, shook hands all around, then followed Raquel toward the door.

Campeche shrugged, stood up, and went to the bar, where he poured himself another drink. "You get anything worth the trip, tiger?" he asked.

Sam smiled. "We'll have to find out," he replied, and as Raquel came back into the room and sank down on the sofa next to Gus Corona, Sam began to read the photostats.

The will had been drawn up about fifteen years ago, but it was a document written in the flowery legal English that was popular a century ago. "I, Cyrus Thurman, being of sound mind, do bequeath to the heirs of my body . . ." He set it aside and picked up the three birth certificates. Albert Thurman was forty-five. Raquel was twenty-five, and Cyrus, Jr., had been twenty-three. There had been two marriages. He looked at the receipt the Mexican attorney had given Sánchez. He went back to the will and found the "certain other documents" attached to the last page. They were photostats of two bills from the Physicians and Surgeons Hospital in Berkeley, both stamped confidential, both stamped paid. Both were for fees paid for the artificial insemination of Mrs. Dorothy Thurman. He looked at the birth certificates again. Both of the hospital bills were dated almost nine months to the day prior to the birth of Raquel Thurman and Cyrus Thurman, Jr. He picked up the will again and reread the first paragraph.

After a while he turned the photostats over in his hand. Along the top of the white side was a small stamp of a Puerto Vallarta photo shop and a date. The photostats had been made ten days earlier.

Antonio Sánchez came into the room and told Raquel that the *criadas* and the cook had returned and wanted to know if *pollo con mole* would be satisfactory for dinner. She reached over, squeezed Gus Corona's hand, then stood up and followed Sánchez down the stairs. The two pilots came up, and Campeche went over to the bar and made them a drink.

"Problems?" Corona asked.

Sam continued studying the photostats. "I think we can overcome it," he replied.

One of the pilots turned on a radio, and the room was filled with the plaintive sounds of a Mexican trio singing a ballad. Corona stood up and stretched. "There's a lot of money involved, isn't there, Sam?" he said casually.

"I honestly don't know, Gus."

"A reporter asked me an interesting question the other day. He asked who was going to get Junior's share of the estate."

Sam nodded. "That all depends on whether or not Junior left a will." He put down the papers and looked toward the detective speculatively. "Why?" he asked.

Corona shrugged. "Being a cop makes a man suspicious." He drifted toward the bar.

Sam turned toward Campeche. "How difficult would it be to get a list of the telephone calls made by Thurman to the United States within the past three weeks?"

"*Mañana*, tiger," Campeche replied. "Tomorrow."

Sam picked up the photostats and looked at the stamp again. "*Fotografía por Martínez*," he said. "Do you think we could check this photo shop and see how many copies he made of these papers?"

"*Mañana*, likewise, tiger." He chuckled softly. "Gus tells me you are one hell of an attorney," he said presently. "I figure you must be if you have the two best detectives in two countries working for you." He chuckled again and upended his tequila.

8

$\mathcal{T}$HE BULKY BROWN envelope with the bloodstained square of cloth was delivered to the *Examiner* in the early-evening pickup of the mail. A headline from an earlier edition of the *Chronicle* had been clipped out and pasted to a piece of wrapping paper. ASTRO STRIKES AGAIN.

The city editor once again notified Homicide that the Astro was bragging of his crime, and approximately a half-hour later Lieutenant Lars Burton appeared in the city room to pick up the evidence.

"This time it was mailed from Oakland," the city editor said, "and there is no code message."

"Yeah, it's strange," Burton said. "Maybe he's going off his rocker."

The city editor shook his head. "You're sick," he said, giving him the package.

Burton took the cloth square back to the police laboratory, where technicians quickly matched it to the fabric of the sarape worn by Thurman. The square was about a quarter of the size of the one that had been taken from the victim's garment. Burton sighed and went into the Homicide Division. Saxeby still was being followed. His movements had a definite pattern. He departed for work regularly, left for home at the same time every day. He stopped at a supermarket on Noriega on his way home, picked up a television dinner and a six-pack of beer. When the new edition of *Astrology Magazine* had appeared on the newsstands, he bought a copy. At no time had he gone to Oakland. A relief linotype operator who had been a former police officer had been set up in the printing plant where Saxeby worked and he reported that Saxeby was an astrology nut and would discuss it with anyone who brought up the subject. He would not mingle with his fellow workers. The only day he had reported sick was the day after the murders, when he had gone to the Marina District.

There was a holdup with a fatal shooting in the Mission District, and Burton went out on this. It was routine. A young man had tried to rob a liquor store and was shot fatally by the proprietor. It was the fourth time the operator had beaten away holdup artists. Burton wondered when some customer would reach in his pocket for a handkerchief and get shot by the proprietor. He already had earned the nickname of Matt Dillon. Burton waited until the photographers had finished and then returned to his car. The hearse was waiting, and soon the attendants pushed their way through the crowd, carrying the victim on a stretcher. The dead man wore Mexican straw shoes with ripple soles that pushed out from under the blanket. Burton belched, then took out his notebook and made a brief entry. The shoes reminded him of the murder victim in the Marina. The girl who had survived the Astro attack, which proved fatal to her boyfriend, had stated that the killer just appeared at the window of the car and fired. In the Astro killing at Golden Gate Park, there had been no sound other than gunfire. In the Marina District there had been footsteps, leather heels with metal tips, and whoever wore them walked briskly before and after the killing.

Whistling softly, he drove away from the holdup scene, crossed Market Street to Bush up to Van Ness. Here he stopped at a lunchroom called the Hippo, where he accepted a free cup of coffee from the manager, whom he considered a friend. A little after six, he left the lunchroom and drove to an imposing three-story home in the Marina District, about a block back from the waterfront.

He clucked softly as he pushed the doorbell. The house probably was worth a hundred thousand, yet it carried a dollar-ninety-eight lock on the front door that could be opened with a piece of celluloid. The door was opened on a chain, and he took out his badge and held it up. "May I come in for a moment?" he said.

The woman nodded, closed the door to release the chain, then opened it wide. "I am Lieutenant Lars Burton," he said.

"I am Mrs. Althea Beldon Thurman," the woman replied. "Is it about this dreadful business?" Her voice was articulate and patronizing, but it did not go with her body. She had large breasts, and she had bent her shoulders forward so long to hide them that she appeared to be permanently round-shouldered. She probably was under forty, but she still wore a girdle. Her hair was cut too short, and her mouth was small. "Is your husband at home?" he asked.

"I expect him any minute." Reluctantly she opened the door wider and motioned for him to come in.

"We are concerned over the whereabouts of his sister," Burton said, removing his hat as he stepped past her. The living room was heavily furnished. A television set was the center of attention. A small cross hung on the wall. "In view of what has been going on, they just asked me to stop by and make sure everything was all right, ma'am."

She shut the door and motioned for him to sit down, then sat across from him. "The Colonel has been playing golf with General Sharp," she said. "I believe his sister is in Mexico."

"Mexico?" he asked, wondering once again how Gus Corona had wangled that junket.

"She went down with her lawyer in an attempt to get control of her father's estate," she said. "She even postponed the funerals."

Burton shook his head sympathetically. "It's terrible," he said. "That happening to your father-in-law, so close, and your not even knowing it."

"I don't believe you were sent here to commiserate with me," she said, folding her arms across her chest.

"Excuse me, ma'am. They just wanted me to check and see that everything is all right."

"You may report to your superiors that everything is satisfactory." She stood up, her arms still folded across her chest.

Burton rose and nodded respectfully. "If you go to Mexico, would you let us know?"

"We shall not be going there," she said.

Again he nodded. "I hope you don't lose out on the estate in any way."

"The Colonel anticipated this and took care of it before she arrived there," she replied, walking ahead of him toward the door. She pulled it open. "Now, really, I think you have accomplished your mission."

"No disrespect intended, ma'am," Burton said as he bobbed his head and stepped past her. At the foot of the stairs he turned and looked up. She still remained in the doorway. "You didn't hear either the car accident or the gunshots that night?" he asked mildly.

"Not a sound, officer. The house is soundproofed and air-conditioned. What is your name again, please?"

"Lars Burton, ma'am." Tipping his hat, he returned to his car.

Sam Benedict awoke late. It was late by his watch, which read nine, and then, because of the time change, he realized that it was two hours later than this. The bed was comfortably hard, the way he liked a bed, and for a little while he relaxed in it, enjoying the comfort that comes with the knowledge that one does not have to get up immediately. He stretched, and when he heard someone murmur outside the window, he swung out of bed and pulled open the heavy draperies. Two floors below him was a kidney-shaped swimming pool. In lounge chairs on the flagstoned patio were Raquel, Gus Corona, and the Mexican detective. Raquel's suit was a ribbon across her chest and loins. The two detectives wore identical shorts, which meant they had either been into the town or there was a supply of swimming trunks maintained in the house. Beyond the patio was a small gate separating the pool area from the beach below. The ocean was the clearest blue, so blue that it was impossible to see a horizon. A dolphin's fin cut the water in a lazy loop, and then, just as he was about to turn away, a huge manta ray shot high out of the water and fell back with a large splash. Sam sighed and wished he could stay a month. A *criada* came out on the patio carrying a tray of *pan dulce* and a large pot of coffee with some cups.

A thought occurred to him, and he crossed to the dresser and opened the drawers. In one was a toothbrush and an extra tube of toothpaste. In another drawer were three pair of trunks identical to those worn by the detectives, and he found that one pair fit comfortably.

He walked down the two flights of stairs, past a large kitchen, and out to the patio. The girl wiggled her fingers toward him, and he wondered how even this minor movement failed to dislodge the rib-

84

bon across her breasts. She probably was one of the most sensual women he ever had seen, and he sighed again, feeling a twinge of pity for Gus Corona.

"Good morning, tiger," Campeche said lazily. He seemed even bigger in trunks and the daylight. There was no fat on his huge body. There was almost a feline attitude in the manner in which he lay on the strap lounge, like a jaguar before he had been skinned to lie on the floor of a Mexican villa.

"The two Carters went into Puerto Vallarta," Raquel said, sitting up. The ribbon remained in its proper position. "They said they would be back about one."

He remembered. Both of the pilots were named Carter, although they were no relation.

"We have all the copies of the photostats," Campeche said. "Would you like some coffee, tiger?"

"I'll get it." He poured some coffee—black, aromatic Mexican coffee—into a large cup, sat down on another lounge, and sipped it.

"There was one telephone call to San Francisco that was completed, and another that was person-to-person that was not," Campeche said, picking up a small notebook from the table next to him. "The one that was not completed was to a David Beldon. The other was to a MI 6-4532."

"Which is the number for my stepbrother," Raquel said.

Sam glanced at Corona and noticed a quick tired look flicker through the detective's eyes. Then he noticed the girl direct her attention away from Corona to him.

"We were discussing the will before you came down," she said. "The way it's written, I will get nothing and Junior would have got nothing, isn't that right?"

"Not necessarily."

"Why not?"

"Any will can be contested," Sam said. "And when did you read the will?"

"This morning. Señor Campeche showed me the photostats, and I read the other papers also. The first paragraph in Daddy's will states that he bequeaths to the heirs of his body. Junior and I were artificially inseminated."

"This has relatively minor significance." Sam took another sip of the delicious black Mexican coffee. "I am sure it was not the intent of your father to cut you out of your inheritance," he said presently. "That introduction to the will was merely a popular legal phrase that preceded the use of artificial insemination. The attorney who drew up the will got his degree three-quarters of a century ago."

"Win some, lose some," she said flippantly.

"Where are the photostats now?"

"In the desk drawer. I locked it and have the key."

"But not on you," Gus said.

She laughed, and Sam thought that lasting grief was indeed only for the old. He buttered one of the hard-crusted Mexican rolls and bit into it. The butter was sweet and tasty.

Raquel stood up and began to tuck her long hair under a bathing cap.

"You going to dive in in that outfit, honey?" Campeche asked.

She looked toward him. "Why not?"

"It will come right off."

A trace of a smile spread across her full lips. "That all depends upon who is in the pool," she said, and turning, she looked provocatively at Gus Corona. Then, with hips swaying, she walked to the edge of the pool and dived in. The suit did not come off.

About three in the afternoon Lars Burton received another call from the city editor of the *Chronicle*. There had been another communication from the Astro, this one accompanied by the usual

86

doggerel and astrological charts. Another half-hour passed, and Lars Burton once again was in the city room of the newspaper. The chart was similar to the others, a crudely drawn circle bisected with degrees and various astrological terms which Burton did not understand. The only thing he knew about astrology was that the Astro was interested in it, and according to a radio commercial for a hit show, that this was the age of Aquarius. The verse was printed in block letters on the usual lined paper.

> ONE OUT OF THREE WILL SEEM
> FAIR TO ME 'TIS THE END OF
> SUCH COMPANY.

The reporter who talked to him was named Kennedy, and he had a strong New England accent. "Does it mean anything to you at all?"

Burton belched slightly as he carefully slid the two pieces of paper back into the envelope in which they had arrived. He noted that they had been mailed the day before. "Gus Corona'd have a better idea, Doug. He should be back tomorrow or the next day."

"Where did he go?"

Burton shook his head. "I don't know."

"Is he working on the Astro?"

Again the paunchy detective shook his head. "Nobody tells me anything. I'll give you a call if I find out anything. I might as well get some publicity out of this too."

The reporter nodded. "Well, you'll have your picture in the paper tomorrow along with the new rhyme," he replied, "if there's room." He went out of the small room ahead of the detective.

Burton smiled dourly and went down the stairs to his patrol car that he had double-parked on Mission Street. He never would be able to understand newspapermen, he thought. If you tried to give them something, they were not interested. If you told him they could not have it, they worried at it like a hungry dog. An actress would not say a word or let her picture be taken, and they hid in the bushes to get her. Another couldn't get a mention if she ran naked through the streets. He picked up the microphone and called in. It was four thirty. There was nothing other than a request to call the deputy chief by line whenever it was convenient.

He drove over to Market Street, made an illegal left turn, and drove up to the Fox Plaza before he found a parking spot convenient to a public telephone in a bar. The chief sounded bored. There had been a complaint against Burton by a Colonel Albert Thurman, who said that Burton had been insolent to his wife the preceding evening.

"It's in the report."

"I read it. He wanted you reprimanded and disciplined, so consider yourself reprimanded and disciplined."

Burton bought a Coke at the bar, then returned to his car. For a while he sat there uncomfortably, wondering why he drank so many Cokes, and watching the miniskirted secretaries pour out of the Fox Plaza. There was wind, which meant no smog and no fog, and that the girls had to hold on to their hair when they came out onto the street.

The radio dispatcher called him. Raymond Saxeby was not following his regular habit pattern. He had left work fifteen minutes early and had just turned off Lombard into the Marina District. Burton straightened and presently pulled out into the rush-hour traffic and crept over toward the San Francisco Yacht Club. The dispatcher relayed the progress. Saxeby drove around the block three times and apparently had not noticed either car on the tail. Then he had driven to the parking area by the seawall and parked. Now he was just sitting behind the wheel of his car, staring out over the bay.

He was still there a little more than a half-hour later when Burton found one of the tail cars, a combination pickup truck and a car, parked back about two blocks from the water. This detective was young, with long sideburns and very heavy curly hair. "He's just sitting there," he said. "Walk down to the corner and look around, and you can see him."

Burton nodded, parked his car in an empty spot about half a block distant, then walked down to the corner. The wind was cold and blowing spray across the pavement from the swells that disintegrated on the breakwater. Saxeby was too far distant to be anything more than a silhouette, hands resting on top of the driving wheel, chin resting on the hands. Burton strode briskly along the sidewalk. If there was one thing he hated to do, it was to walk briskly, but few persons paid any attention to a man who walked as if he was in a hurry to reach his destination.

Saxeby was parked almost on the spot where the Volkswagen bus had been found. His car was just old enough to be out of place, to be conspicuous in this neighborhood. Burton continued down the block, and then, as he drew closer, Saxeby straightened, cast a disinterested look in his direction, and started the car. Burton caught an impression of sunken cheeks, high cheekbones, and a long pointed chin as the car backed out in a slow turn, then slowly moved away in the direction of Highway 101 and the Golden Gate Bridge. When he turned the corner, a blue Ford sedan backed out of one of the driveways and followed him.

Unlike his previous visit, Saxeby did not head back toward his home. When Burton had returned to his own car, the young detective had disappeared, and Burton soon heard him report that the suspect was crossing the Golden Gate Bridge, heading north.

"Stay with him," Burton said, and yawning, he also turned toward the Golden Gate Bridge.

The unseen Saxeby turned right off the north end of the bridge into a narrow Sausalito road. The slow chase was reported about every fifteen seconds by the trailing police cars, until it stopped for a while at a small waterfront beer bar. Here the tail cars ran into a problem. The road was only two lanes wide, and if one stopped, traffic would be blocked. If they drove out onto the rocks, attendants would want to park their cars. The only possible answer was to park one car in the center of the town and the other about a mile distant in the other direction.

Burton pulled out onto the pier and noticed the bearded parking attendant stiffen when he opened the door and saw the microphone hooked to the dashboard. He gave the attendant two dollars in advance, but the attendant was still nervous as he cautiously backed the car into an empty slot about three cars distant from Saxeby's.

Approximately a dozen persons leaned against the bar, which was made of barrels and red plastic. Another half-dozen couples sat around larger barrels in director's chairs, listening to a young man who was playing a guitar and singing country music. Saxeby was by himself at the end of the bar with a stein of beer in front of him. He did not fit in the tavern any more than did Burton, but he did not appear to be aware of it. He was a very thin man. He wore Levis and a blue shirt, and his unshined black shoes had rippled soles.

Burton ordered a stein of bock beer. Someone in the place was smoking pot. There was enough smoke to make everyone high. He sipped from his beer. The parking attendant came in, dropped some coins in a cigarette machine, then walked over to the bartender and whispered in his ear.

The bartender nodded, passed the boy a packet of matches, then drew a glass of beer, and carried it over to the boy with the guitar. The boy continued to sing, but the song changed. Burton caught a few words, such as "establishment" and "fuzz." In less than five minutes the only patrons inside the tavern were Saxeby and himself.

"Quieted down real sudden," Saxeby said after a while to the bartender.

"It goes like that. Up and down." The bartender wiped the counter in front of him. "Live here?"

Saxeby shook his head. "Frisco," he replied, apparently unaware that his answer showed he was new to the area. No one who lived here called San Francisco "Frisco." His voice was midwestern-nasal. The bartender sighed and turned away, then leaned against the back bar, hands folded across his chest. "How do you get to Portola Avenue?" Saxeby asked.

"First traffic light, turn left, then go up the hill," the bartender replied. "You'll run right into it."

It took Lars Burton a few minutes to remember why the name of the street was familiar, and then he recalled this was the avenue on which Raquel Thurman lived. He finished his beer and went back to his car. When he was well away from the tavern, he called dispatch for the number, had them notify the two tail cars, and then drove on up the hill. The house was easy to find. A mailbox outside had the number on it. A Porsche was parked on the planked carport. He drove past it, turned up an S turn into a higher hill, then used another carport to turn around. He found a place to park that was partially off the street and near a large clump of willows growing out of the hillside. Sausalito, he thought. It meant "little willow" in Spanish. Through the willows he could look directly down upon the carport and entrance to Raquel Thurman's house.

A little more than an hour passed before Saxeby left the tavern. It was dark, and the lights of Belvedere, Tiburon, and San Francisco were reflected in long vivid moving streamers across the waters of the bay. The young detective, the boy driving the combination car and pickup truck, noticed Saxeby as he turned up the hill. He reported it, and presently Burton saw shafts from the headlights slowly coming up the hill. They swung around the abrupt turn before her house, slowed almost imperceptibly as they passed, then continued on up the hill. Burton swore softly and slid way down in his seat, at the same time shutting off the radio.

Saxeby went about three houses farther up the hill than had Burton before he turned around and came back down. He parked on the banked shoulder of the road in front of Raquel Thurman's house. When Burton heard the engine die, he straightened in his seat, turned the radio on softly, and took the night binoculars from their case. Saxeby remained in his car, hands once again curled over the top of the steering wheel. For almost an hour he held the same pose, and Burton wondered if possibly he had gone to sleep. When he finally moved, he moved quickly. The door opened, was shut silently, and then he ran across the narrow road to the carport. Here he crouched behind the coupé, barely visible in the night glasses, for another long period before he suddenly, with a furtive movement, slithered down a small flight of steps to the front entrance. Here he paused for a brief second; then, turning, he bolted up the stairs and raced across the street. With no attempt at secrecy, he turned on his headlights and let the car roll forward as he started it. The tires screeched on the first turn.

"He's coming down, and fast," Burton said into the microphone, then let his police car roll down to the same spot where Saxeby had parked.

Carrying a flashlight, Burton walked across the street and down the flight of stairs. The front door to the home had been battered open. Jagged shards of wood angled out from the doorjamb, and the planking on the door had been ruptured. The interior of the house was dark. He put out the flashlight and moved to one side of the partially open door, knowing that it would do no good if someone was inside with a gun. A bullet that passed through thin wood first was just as fatal as one that did not. He was out of his jurisdiction, but the Sausalito cops were friendly. There was no car parked anywhere around that looked out of place. He burped heavily, tasting beer, then took out his gun and pushed the door open wider with his foot. Holding his flashlight out far from his body, he took a deep breath, turned it on, and walked into the house. It seemed empty and neat.

He turned on a lamp next to a sofa on which there was a telephone with a long extension cord. Nothing appeared out of order. It had not been ransacked. He moved into the next room, a bedroom and very feminine. There was no one under the bed or in the closets. The same was true in the next bedroom, although there was a suitcase under the queen-sized bed that startled him for a second. He returned to the first bedroom and found a long narrow jewelry box on top of the dresser. He was no expert on jewelry, but the white stones in four or five pieces looked like diamonds. He lifted out a tray. Two hundred-dollar bills rested on the velvet cushion. It had been no robber who kicked the door down.

Another thought suddenly occurred to him, and he went back to the second bedroom and pulled out the suitcase from under the bed. It was a medium-small Samsonite case with latches that pushed down into the bag molding. An airline baggage tag was strapped around the handle which bore the letters SFO. The handle was covered by a corrugated leather that would carry no prints, so it would be safe to move it. Picking it up, he started toward the door, then paused as he heard another car coming up the grade, moving fast. It could be rather embarrassing if he was seen carrying a suitcase across the street, since he was out of his jurisdiction.

The car slowed before it rounded the curve, and Burton remembered there were no houses there. It started to speed up, then braked abruptly and backed up.

He dropped the suitcase in the middle of the floor and moved quickly into the girl's bedroom. The car outside squealed into the carport platform, and then steps crackled down the stairs.

The steps paused by the open door. "I recognized your car," a voice said.

Lars Burton put his gun away and belched again, as he stepped out of the bedroom. Corona, wearing a white open-necked shirt, looked as tanned as if he had been in the sun for a month.

More steps slowly came down the stairs behind him, and Raquel appeared. She was dressed in brown leather, knee-high boots, jacket, and short skirt. She paused, and her eyes widened as she saw the smashed door. "You could have had a key," she said, moving into the room. She paused again, and her eyes opened wider when she saw the suitcase.

"Is it your father's?" Burton asked.

She nodded slowly. "I think so," she said. "But it was stolen." She shivered and moved closer to Corona, who gently placed his arm around her.

"Did you look under the bed?"

Again she nodded, then shook her head. "I don't know."

"What brought you out?" Corona said mildly.

Burton shrugged. "One of the suspects was tailed over here. When he saw the forcible entry, he left."

Corona looked down at the girl. "Open it, honey," he said quietly.

The girl moved away from him, picked up the suitcase, and placed it on the sofa. It was not locked. She took out some shorts, shirts, three pair of socks, an extra pair of pants, and finally a soft leather briefcase. She glanced nervously toward the splintered door, as if fearful of being caught doing something wrong, then sat down next to the open suitcase and unzipped the briefcase.

Burton drifted behind the sofa and looked over her shoulder. She first took out a lined tablet of yellow paper. On the top, someone had written in a strong upright hand, "Antonio Sánchez—100,000; María Delgado—100,000." Below this were scribbled a half-dozen telephone numbers with the area codes in front of them. One was New York, the others in San Francisco.

Placing the tablet on the sofa, she rummaged in the briefcase again and took out a thick envelope made of cardboard. Printed on one side were the words "Last Will & Testament of Cyrus Thurman, Sr." It was held together by a braided elastic band. She looked at it for a moment, then dug into the briefcase again. She went into it the way a woman goes into a purse, looking inside and pulling out the contents one by one. A man, Burton thought, would have upended the contents on the sofa.

An unsealed manila envelope came out. She opened it, and he saw what appeared to be two receipts from the Physicians and Surgeons Hospital for a payment of some sort. The final item in the case was a plain white envelope. When she opened this, a check fell out, drawn on the Bank of America. It was made out to Cyrus Thurman, Jr., in the amount of one thousand dollars.

Tears suddenly brimmed in the girl's eyes, and she wiped at the corners with her index finger.

Gus Corona bent over, picked up the papers, and slipped them back into the briefcase. "Why don't you look around, honey, and see if anything is missing," he suggested gently.

She looked blankly around the living room, then went into the bedroom.

"Where did you find the suitcase?" Corona asked.

"Under the bed in the other bedroom," Burton said, taking out a roll of antacid tablets and popping one in his mouth. "If I remember the reports right, it was missing."

"You remember right."

Burton nodded toward the door. "What are you going to do about that?"

"She'll report it, and we'll get it nailed up."

The girl came back into the living room. "Nothing appears to be missing," she said. Her voice was steady, although her eyes still glistened from the tears. "I am going to call Sam."

Burton turned toward the door. "I'll write it up," he said; then, nodding toward the girl, he went out of the house. When he got back to the car, he picked up the binoculars and aimed them through the open door of the house below. The girl was just turning away from the telephone, and she moved right into the arms of Gus Corona, who was standing behind her, her head resting on his shoulder. Burton dropped the night glasses back into their case. When he had been young, he had never made out on a case, but it seemed like Corona could never miss.

He started the car and slowly let it roll down the hill and around the hairpin turn. The door was still wide open when he went past the house, but Corona and the girl were out of sight. Corona was a hell of a good cop, Lars Burton thought, slowly coasting down the steep hill, but the odds were good that if he ever got hit, he would not have his pants on. As he turned the next curve, he slowed and looked at San Francisco across the bay. The lights of the distant city painted a bright foreground to the full moon rising over the horizon.

He picked up the microphone and asked for a report. Saxeby had driven at high speed directly to his home in the Sunset District and presumably was in bed.

9

BOTH FUNERALS were held four days after Cyrus Thurman was killed, one at ten in the morning for Cyrus Thurman, Sr., and the other for his son at two in the afternoon. Sam Benedict had been unable to attend either one, but about two hours after the second, Trudy Black announced on the intercom that Gus Corona had arrived.

Sam pushed aside his papers and leaned back in his chair as the detective came into the room and sprawled into the easy chair in front of the desk. "There are a few items of interest," he said, taking a small notebook from his inside jacket pocket. "Aside from the press and Raquel, there were only two persons who attended both services. One was Stella Ross, who was Thurman's first wife."

"I want to talk to her," Sam said. "Raquel has told me she did not know where she lived."

Corona nodded. "Raquel did not get a chance to talk to her, but we got the license number of the car she drove. It's registered to a Milton Ross in Los Gatos."

"Good." The thought flickered through his mind that he should set up Corona in business and use him for all of his investigative work. "Who was the other?" he asked.

"Our prime suspect as the Astro, Raymond Saxeby, and man, is he weird. He didn't take his eyes away from Raquel once during both services. He had that real hungry look a man gets when he hasn't been laid for a long time and he really needs it."

Sam tipped back farther in his chair and placed his feet on the desk. "It doesn't follow the Astro's pattern. In the past he has killed at random, and he has never raped any of his victims."

"But there is a sex hang-up. With his female victims, he has cut off their bras or panties and scissored a piece from them to send along with his charts and poetry to the papers."

"We'd better get her out of that house."

"She won't go."

Sam clasped his hands behind his head. "Anything else?"

"Yeah. The Colonel got her aside and said that she was making a mistake having a man with your reputation as her attorney. He told her you would wind up with anything she might be able to get out of the estate."

Sam smiled. "And what did she say?"

"She was real cool. She said she hadn't discovered that your fees were particularly exorbitant, and if you were good enough for her father, you were good enough for her."

Sam was pleased. There was nothing a lawyer liked more than to have the complete confidence of his client. "I'm certainly grateful for your help, Gus," he said aloud.

The lanky detective stood up and dropped the address of Milton Ross on the desk. "I've got a personal interest in this case," he said.

Sam stood up and followed him to the door, shook hands, returned to his desk, and buzzed for Trudy. She came in immediately, glasses raised on top of her thick black hair. "Mr. Howard Dredge called," she said as she walked across the room carrying her notebook. "He sounded upset about your trip to Mexico, and he suggested a round-table conference between all the Thurmans and you and him to reach some sort of a settlement." She sat down in her chair and opened her shorthand book.

"Why don't you call him back and set up the conference here," he said thoughtfully. "But before you set that up, try to get an appointment with Mrs. Milton Ross." He gave her the slip of paper that Corona had left. "Make it at her convenience, and cancel anything else in the way."

He watched her go out of the room, hips swaying, then closed his eyes and tried to recall Howard Dredge. He could not paint a mental picture of the man, but from somewhere he recalled that he had graduated from Stanford, worked as a law clerk in the old firm of David Beldon, been made a partner, and eventually had acquired the practice after Beldon died.

The intercom came on. "Mrs. Ross has just returned from a funeral and feels like hell," Trudy said. "She'll be over it tomorrow and will see you anytime after noon."

Stella Ross lived in a large house in the hills on the outskirts of Los Gatos about fifty miles south of the city. They passed through an open gate, guarded by two large stone cats, and up a wide asphalt driveway for almost three-quarters of a mile before they came to the house. She came to the door herself. She was a buxom woman in her late forties or early fifties, and the high-necked lounging pajamas and mules she wore seemed out of place in this setting. Her voice was low and rasping.

"What the hell," she said, "if Sam Benedict will drive all the way from San Francisco, there is probably a reason for it." She ushered them into a living room that was basic red.

"Trudy Black," Sam said, "my assistant."

"Of course," she replied. "If I had known you were bringing a chaperon, I'd have worn the widow's weeds. What will you have to drink?"

"It's a little early."

Stella Ross shrugged and sat down in a chair. "I read that you were handling Cy's business." She lit a cigarette. "What do you want to know?"

Trudy took out her shorthand book and a ball-point pen. Stella Ross glanced toward her and shrugged again. "Can you tell me why you and Cy Thurman were divorced?" Sam asked.

An impish smile spread over her face, and once again she looked toward Trudy. "There was the usual jazz about mental cruelty, but the real reason was that Cy couldn't get a hard-on and Milt Ross couldn't get off one for more than thirty minutes."

Sam grinned. Trudy did not change her expression as her pen scribbled along the lined notebook. "Is Albert your son by Cy?" Sam asked.

She sighed. "How about that?" she replied. "It was the one and only time he wasn't like limp macaroni, and I got caught. I was so surprised that I forgot to take care of myself."

"Was he a homosexual?"

"Hell, no. There was nothing faggy about Cy. We took care of each other in other ways, really," she replied, dragging on her cigarette. "He just had a problem that he couldn't quite get it hard enough. He got over it later on, apparently, because he had two kids by Dorothy. She was a dainty little thing. Maybe I just came on too strong."

"Do you see Albert often?"

"Hell, no. He's scared to death I'll say 'shit' or something in

front of one of his officers." She bent forward and snubbed the cigarette out in an ashtray. "Who is your client, Raquel or Al?"

"Raquel Thurman."

"I hadn't seen her for maybe twenty years. She is as good-
looking a wench as the picture in the papers showed."

"She's very attractive."

Stella Ross lit another cigarette and leaned back in her chair.
"Sounds like there may be a fight between the two of them over Cy's
estate. Didn't Cy leave a will?"

Sam nodded. "But it appears that there may be some litigation over the interpretation of some of the clauses." He picked an invisible thread from his pants. "Albert seems to be pretty well off
financially."

"He married some real bitch for her dough, but I don't know
how much she had. He likes money. Even as a kid, he liked money."

"How was that?"

"Cy gave him an allowance of ten bucks a week. He was paid
it on Sunday, and he was always broke by Thursday. I suppose that's
why he joined the military. He couldn't take care of himself without
being on some kind of a welfare project."

"Did Cy give you an income as a part of the divorce pro-
ceedings?"

"Nope. He gave me a cash settlement and this house. Milt is a
stockbroker, and we've boosted the settlement up pretty good. Cy
was a great guy. They have never come any better." Again she
dragged deeply on her cigarette. "But you didn't come all the way
down here just to chitchat."

Sam smiled. "As a matter of fact, that is why I came down,
Mrs. Ross. There were a couple of other factors. It was a nice day to
get out of the office. And I wanted to find out if you had heard from
Cy recently."

"I received a letter from him a few weeks ago saying he was
coming back for a few days and that he would probably call. Before

that, I hadn't heard from him since about a week before he went away. Of course, he and Milt were in touch with each other regularly. Milt handled some stock investments for him."

Sam sighed slowly. The name Milton Ross was in his files on Cyrus Thurman, listed as the stockbroker for Thurman. He had not connected the names.

"He didn't write to Milt about his visit," Stella Ross continued, "so it didn't have anything to do with him."

Outside, a horn was blown, and he heard the sound of a car coming up the driveway. "Did Cy give any reason as to why he was coming back when he wrote to you?" Sam asked.

"No. He just said he had some minor business to look after, that it was no big deal, and that if he could work it, he would like to get together." She stood up as the car came to a stop outside and moved toward the door. "If the cops were half as efficient as they claim to be, they would have caught that goddamn Astro by now."

"They'll get him," Sam said.

Stella Ross left the room. A door slammed, and she returned presently with a man about ten years older than she. He was balding, wore steel-rimmed spectacles, and was very short and very thin. "This is my husband, Milton Ross," Stella said proudly.

The man acknowledged the introduction in a voice as deep as a bass viol.

"Did you handle all of Thurman's investments?" Sam asked Ross.

"I believe I did. He didn't do much trading, and most of it is in blue chips."

"What do you think he was worth?"

"I know what he was worth in stocks, debentures, and bonds because I had a tally run after his murder. It comes to just under three million dollars. Add in his house in Puerto Vallarta, and I would estimate he would cash out a little more than three million."

"Did you do this on your own volition, or did someone ask you to?"

"I was asked to do so by an attorney named Howard Dredge who is representing the Colonel. I have sent him a list, and I will send you one also if you wish me to do so."

"I do indeed."

"I was called by Dredge today," Stella Ross said. "He said there is a possibility that I may have to testify briefly in the probate court."

"What's the beef?" Ross asked. "A man of your stature doesn't come all the way down here as a matter of routine."

"He wanted to know if I was Albert's mother, honey," Stella Ross said. "It's no big deal."

"With Sam Benedict everything is a big deal," Ross replied. "I don't know what you are planning, and I don't care, except that I don't want either you or Dredge putting Stella on any grill."

"That's my man," Stella said fondly.

Sam stood up and held out his hand. "I don't think you or Mrs. Ross will have any problem."

"Good." Ross's grip was extraordinarily strong. "I'll send over that list of Cy's stock holdings tomorrow."

A short time later, when they were driving back to the city, Trudy suddenly giggled. "She's funny," she explained later. "From her description of Milton Ross, I had painted a mental picture of a man about the size of a gorilla."

Sam laughed softly and reached over and touched Trudy gently on the thigh. "You'll just have to take her word for it," he said.

She patted the back of his hand. "Why don't we stop and have that drink it was too early for, when we get to San Jose?"

He nodded and settled down more comfortably in his seat.

"Why are you trying to throw out the will, Sam?" she asked quietly.

At times Trudy was like a wife. She anticipated him, or perhaps she had extrasensory perception. There had been more than one occasion when he had thought he would like a cup of coffee and a moment later she appeared and placed one on his desk. She had a legal mind as well as the mind of a psychic. "Our client probably was the result of an artificial impregnation," he replied. "The will was written by an old man who used language that was the vogue before anyone ever heard of artificial insemination: 'to the heirs of my body.' Thus, if Raquel Thurman is to get her fair share of the estate of the late Cyrus Thurman, the will probably will have to be invalidated. There were two witnesses when the testator signed the document. One was Beldon's secretary, who died about a year after he did, and the other was Althea Thurman, who was the granddaughter of David Beldon."

"Is she a good witness?"

Sam nodded. "That's one way to approach the problem. As the only living witness, we can call upon her to prove the will. Usually a witness to the authenticity of the will is prohibited from taking any property under the will. Althea Thurman is not named as an heir, but she is the wife of an heir, and the point certainly is raised that under community property she is at least half-an-heir." He smiled again. "I imagine Dredge has thought of this. If she testifies, her husband runs the risk of losing any part of the inheritance, yet he wants to grab the entire thing. Now, if she doesn't testify, they run the risk of having the will thrown out."

"Which puts us in a rather strong position," Trudy said.

"The most logical thing to do is to divide it up evenly, as Cy certainly wanted it."

"And yet Dredge gives every indication that he is going to contest it."

"For a man in the Colonel's position, there isn't that much difference between one and a half million and three million."

"Maybe he needs the money," Trudy said.

Suddenly he was struck by the sensation that something was barely eluding him. An answer hung just out of sight in the back of his mind. In a courtroom or in his office he would have been able to force it into conscious thought, but in the fast highway traffic, his driving demanded too much attention. He was not concerned. Whatever it was would come back to him. It always did. He concentrated on Trudy's comment. This had not triggered his mental reaction, and he wondered if there could be a reason why a colonel would need such a large sum of money. Stella Ross had described him as being "on the welfare" all of his life. He had been graduated from Occidental College in Los Angeles, been given a commission in the Army, and sent to Vietnam when the United States first became involved in the conflict. The house in the Marina had been purchased about a decade ago because, according to Raquel, it was in a "socially acceptable district and close to the Presidio." The houses there cost money, a minimum of one hundred thousand.

"No matter how much you have, it's not enough," Trudy said. "Look at Howard Hughes."

Sam chuckled. "An excellent client would be Mr. Hughes," he replied, putting the case aside for the day.

Fourteen days after the murder of Cyrus Thurman, Sr., Raymond Saxeby once again deviated from his usual routine. When he left the print shop, he drove in the stop-and-go lanes of traffic to the main post office on Mission Street. One of the men in the tail car unobtrusively followed him into the building, entering just as Saxeby turned away from the main letter drop and headed back toward the parking area. The detective purchased some stamps from an automatic machine and followed Saxeby back into the parking lot. A moment later they were trailing him once again toward the general direction of the Sunset District. The detective reported the incident by radio. The postal authorities would be notified, but the letter Saxeby had mailed would most probably never be found.

"That's probably why he mailed it inside instead of at the curb," one of the detectives said.

"Maybe he put a return address on it."

"Yeah. He might be that dumb."

At Van Ness Avenue, Saxeby turned toward the right instead of going straight. The detectives notified Lars Burton of the variance in the routine, and a few minutes later were notified in turn that Burton was somewhere behind them.

Lars Burton had acquired a much greater understanding of his quarry. He always appeared to be lost in deep thought. He noticed little around him, even to the point of missing stop signs and an occasional traffic light. About a week earlier he had run a red light at Gough Street and Post, and was stopped about a block away by a prowl car. The traffic cop discovered that Saxeby had forgotten his wallet in which he carried his driver's license. The traffic cop had wanted to bring him in, and when told that Saxeby was a leader, he could not resist the temptation to look around to see if he could spot the tail car. Still, Saxeby had not noticed. Another item had been noted by his followers. At the supermarket on Noriega where Saxeby stopped for his beer nightly, he invariably picked up a six-pack from the same spot in the cooler. Space on the shelves was not allocated to any particular brand, so Saxeby drank a different beer almost every night.

This was the first change in his routine since the night he had gone to Sausalito. When Saxeby turned into the Marina District, Burton wondered if there was going to be a repetition of the first procedure across the bridge. It started out the same. Saxeby drove to the same spot at the parking area across from the Yacht Club and parked in the same spot and once again leaned forward, his chin resting on his arms, folded across the wheel. A ray of sun reflected through the window, giving a bluish tint to his thick close-cropped white hair. He remained in this position for a quarter of an hour, then straightened, took a piece of paper from his jacket pocket, read it, placed it beside him on the seat, and started the car.

Instead of heading out of the area toward the bridge, however, he drove the short block to the home of Lieutenant Colonel Albert Thurman. He looked at the paper, looked at the house, then backed up slightly and turned off his engine. Stepping out of the car, he raised the hood, the usual California distress signal, and leaned against the fender, hands folded across his chest. For two or three minutes he remained in this position before he pushed himself away and went up the stairs to ring the doorbell.

Burton belched, removed the safety catch from his gun in its holster, got out of his car, and began to walk briskly down the street. It was Althea Thurman who opened the door. She shook her head, pointed vaguely down the street, then went back into the house and shut the door. For a moment Saxeby hesitated, then turned slowly and went down the stairs. Almost indifferently, he slammed down the hood to his car, got in it, and drove away.

Lars Burton sighed, replaced the safety on his revolver, and returned to his car at a much slower pace.

They called it a bellboy. It was a small plastic box that Gus Corona carried on his belt when he was on duty. Despite its name, the small box emitted a loud electronic whistle rather than a bell whenever someone at the station wanted him to call in. Sometimes the whistle embarrassed him, such as now, when he was with Raquel in the cocktail lounge at the top of the Mark Hopkins Hotel. Although he shut it off quickly, the high whistle carried over the conversation of most of the lounge, shushing it for a few seconds as the patrons looked around to determine where the strange noise was coming from.

When he returned, Raquel had ordered two more tequilas and tonic. Women were clever with their little tricks, he thought, as he slid into the seat. A woman alone in a bar was fair game for any man on the prowl. A woman with an empty seat across from her and a full drink in front of it was not alone. It saved her a lot of trouble. "It was Lars Burton," he said. "He's wondering what happened to the Swedish maid."

Raquel looked at him curiously. "I don't follow you."

"Lars has been going over the reports. During our first discussion you said your father had mentioned that the telephone had been answered by a Swedish maid when he called your half-brother."

"You have a good memory."

"It was all on tapes and was transcribed."

"Oh." She sipped from her drink. "Her name is Astrid Olson, and she's not really a maid, although Althea and Albert usually referred to her as such. It was one of those deals where girls come over from Sweden for a little while to learn English." Her eyes widened suddenly. "What do you mean what happened to her?"

He held up his hand. "It's nothing to get excited about. Lars was just wondering why on at least two occasions Althea has opened her front door herself when she has a maid."

"Who knows why Althea does anything. She's crazy."

"Lars had a Swede down at the station call her. The Colonel answered the phone and said the Olson woman had left their employ about two weeks ago."

"No one would stay with them very long. He's too military, and she's too imbecilic. Why would Lars Burton bother to call you about a thing like that?"

"He thought you might know what happened to her."

"Do you file a report every time you take me out?" She smiled over the rim of her glass.

"Nope. I just passed the word that all queries to you were to be handled personally by me. It was two weeks ago that your father died. It was two weeks ago that Astrid Olson left the Thurmans."

Her smile faded. "I imagine she would have had to register

somewhere, like with the Swedish consulate or the Immigration Department."

"He'll check it out."

"I'm sure he will," she replied thoughtfully. "I imagine there is a hell of a lot of checking out going on that no one ever hears of."

"You know most of it."

"What happened today that made your friend aware that Althea was opening her own door."

Gus smiled. "I really don't know."

"Aren't you curious? Didn't you ask?"

"No." He picked up his drink. "If you're curious, however, I'll ask him. The other things that happened today, that I know of, are that Sam Benedict was out of town this afternoon and that the girl friend of the guy who owned the VW psychedelic bus came in today and tried to get it. She didn't."

Raquel finished her drink. "Shall we?" she said, standing up.

They ate at India House, a small and dark restaurant at the foot of Washington Street near North Beach. The waiters were soft-spoken, turbaned Hindus, the bartender was a Sikh, and their host was Colonial British. The curry was delicate and delicious. Over coffee, she asked for the name of the girl who had tried to recover the Volkswagen.

"Amelia Jones," he replied. "Oddly, it is a name one remembers. Why?"

She began to trace a series of circles on the tablecloth with her well-manicured nail. "Apparently Albert is attracting more than normal interest on behalf of the police," she answered slowly. "This must be because there is some suspicion that he may have been involved in patricide."

"Everyone—"

"Please let me finish," she interrupted. "When Father called Albert, he said only that he would be arriving in Junior's car. But it wasn't Junior's car. It was one he had borrowed. If this was the first time he had borrowed it, then there would have been no way for Albert to have identified it with him. If Father was not the random choice of a psychotic killer, then there must have been some way for the murderer to have recognized Junior's car."

Gus sighed. "Everyone wants to be a cop," he said.

"I am very serious, Gus. You say Father was murdered inside the car."

"What do you want to do?"

"Go see Amelia Jones. She would know how long Junior had been driving the car. Is she living in the commune at the Art Barn?"

"That's the place."

"It's practically within walking distance."

The Art Barn was appropriately named. It overlooked the North Beach area near what had once been the Barbary Coast, but back up on the hill. The sidewalk leading up to it had stairs carved into the cement. The cars on the street, parked at ninety-degree positions to the sidewalk, appeared to be tipped at such an angle that the most gentle push would upend them and send them clattering like bowling pins down into the busy traffic on Broadway.

Gus was winded when they reached the top of the hill. They walked into a small courtyard. The smell of pot was strong even outside the two-story building. Someone who was very good was playing a classical guitar. He slipped his arm through hers, and they walked across the cobbled patio, past a couple of parked Volkswagen buses, and up a short flight of wooden stairs. The door was open. The lights were dim, but there was enough to show that the walls were covered with paintings. At one time the building had been a private home, but a partition had been knocked down to make the lower floor a gallery. Near the rear of the studio, or gallery, steps curved up to a second floor, and it was up there that the guitarist played.

Gus paused when he noticed a young girl, barefoot and wearing skin-tight Levis and a beaded sweater, sitting on a stool near the foot of the stairs. Her hair was long and straight and hung to her waist. "Is Amelia Jones here?" he asked.

The girl stood up, placed her fingers across her lips, then went up the stairs two at a time. Gus looked at Raquel, who shrugged and strolled over to one wall for a closer look at the paintings. Most of them were poorly done nudes or seminudes, he thought, looking around the studio. His eyes were becoming accustomed to the dim light. Many of the canvases were framed, and price tags were tucked in the corners. He noticed one for sale for $450, and the thought occurred to him that some members of this urban commune were indeed materialistic in judging the value of their art.

Raquel seemed to read his mind. "The prices are unreal," she commented as she came over to him.

The music stopped abruptly. A telephone rang several times and then gave up. Gus sighed, then moved along with Raquel as she looked at each of the paintings. One had been sold, apparently. There was a large empty space on the wall, and even in the dim light he could see the darker outline on the wall that had been covered by the painting.

A short but powerfully built man in his middle thirties came down the stairs. His hair was long, and he wore a full beard that he combed with his fingers as he moved. His only visible garment was an orange wraparound skirt that came down to his ankles. "Yes?" he said as he came toward them.

"We're looking for Amelia Jones."

"She's not here." His voice was high and reedy. "If you wish to leave a message, I will give it to her when she returns."

"Who are you?" Gus asked mildly.

"I am no one, because I have not reached my destiny. No one is anyone until he reaches his destiny."

"I am Raquel Thurman," she said. "Junior's sister."

The man bowed slightly. "He has been moved."

"Do you run this place?" Gus asked in his same mild tone.

"This is a haven for those who have the will to seek out their destiny. It is run by no one and by all."

"I think we'll have to move you, too," Gus said. "I'm getting high on the fumes."

The man straightened slightly, and his eyes narrowed. "What are you after?" His voice dropped a half-octave. "I'm clean, and there's no want."

"Amelia Jones."

"That was her on the stairs when you came in. She's gone now. They've all gone. They went out the back way because she pegged you for a fuzz."

"You own this joint?"

"I lease it. I let some kids who can paint hang around. The tourists come in and buy enough." He turned to Raquel. "I'm sorry about your brother. That was a bad scene."

"How often did he drive that psychedelic bus?" Raquel asked.

The man shook his head. "It's only been around a few days. I don't pay any attention. Once he took it to get a model."

"A model?"

"Yeah. Cy had a little talent. He did one good nude of this broad and had just started another. She wasn't a pro, but she liked to take her clothes off. She had a pretty good set of boobs, and I know he banged her a couple of times."

Raquel raised her eyebrows. "Junior?"

"Yeah, Junior. She might of helped him along. I don't know. But they sacked out here a couple of times. Everything's pretty open upstairs."

"I'm glad to hear it," Raquel said. "Where is the painting of her that he finished?"

The man pointed to the blank space on the wall. "Some square came in about a couple of weeks ago and bought it. Paid three hundred and fifty dollars for it. Cy got half, and I got half."

"Where's the one he started?"

"It's gone." The man played with his beard. "When he moved on, the other kids borrowed his canvas and brushes."

"He did more than one and a half paintings," Raquel said. "Where are the others?"

"Some were sold. There are two or three others around." He nodded toward the distant wall, then led them across the room. He pointed out four.

Gus did not understand them. All were a series of lines and angles and cubes. "They don't bear any signature," Raquel said.

"He didn't sign any of his stuff."

"Was the nude that was sold an abstraction?"

The man shook his head. "It was a real portrait. The kid was good."

"Who bought it?" Gus asked.

The man shrugged. "Some tourist. An average-sized guy. He spent a long time here just looking around, then he bought it with cash. At first I thought he was a cop."

"Mind if we look around upstairs?"

Again the man shrugged his shoulders and turned toward the stairs. The upper floor was divided into two sections, one partitioned off into studios, the other a large room with very little light and with a half-dozen double-bed mattresses scattered around the floor. There was a rear door at the end of the corridor which opened onto a flight of stairs leading back to the street below. "Like I said, man, everyone has left."

"Junior didn't live here," Raquel said, touching one of the mattresses with the point of her shoe.

The proprietor shook his head. "I don't think he ever spent a night here. He had a pad somewhere close by. Amelia would know. She stayed with him sometimes."

Gus Corona took a card from his wallet and gave it to the man. "You tell Amelia I would like to speak to her tomorrow and to call me," he said.

"Sure, if she comes around."

"If she doesn't come around, make sure she gets the word."

Raquel talked steadily on the drive back to Sausalito, one hand resting intimately on his thigh. Junior always had been the delicate child, but the lovable one. She had never known Albert very well, although he came to visit them when they were living in Orinda. Albert always had been very formal, and he loved to wear his uniform. Junior had always seemed effeminate, and although no one ever had said anything about it, she had thought that he might be a homosexual. He had never been drafted and he had never explained why he had not been called up. It was hard to believe what the man had said.

"Don't believe it," Gus said.

"I want to. I'm woman enough to want a man to be a man."

He laughed. "I try to oblige." He turned into the carport, held the door for her to get out of the car, then opened the front door to the house with the key he had kept for the new lock.

Raquel bent down, picked up the letters that had been slipped through the mail slot, turned on the light, and began sorting them as she walked on into the room. Most of them were bills, and she tossed them on the sofa, then tore the end off one in her hand. Gus noticed the puzzled expression that flickered over her face as she passed it to him. It was a rectangular piece of green poster paper. A crudely shaped heart was pasted near the top, and typewritten below were the words "I love you. It is predestined."

"A child's Valentine in May?" she asked.

Gus Corona looked at the envelope. The address was typewritten in an uneven line. The third stem of the "m" in "Thurman" was missing, as it was in all of the other letters written by the Astro. "You're going to move out of here," he said quietly.

Her expression became more serious. "What does it mean?"

"I don't know what it means, but you have attracted the attention of the Astro." He pointed out the missing stem, then explained its significance.

She paled, but when she spoke, her voice was even. "I don't believe it. It doesn't make sense." She turned her back to him and raised her heavy hair from her shoulders to her head. "Unzip me," she asked.

He pulled down the zipper; then, putting his hands around her, he cupped her breasts and presently felt the nipples grow hard in his palms. The skin on her back was velvet smooth. She let her hair fall back down, placed her hands over his, and pressed against him. "Nothing will happen so long as you are here," she said softly.

He agreed silently. It was when he was not with her that he feared for her.

10

SAM BENEDICT was the last one to enter the room. The meeting was held in what Trudy referred to as the board room, and Sam had never been able to figure out whether the designation came from the fact that all four walls of the room were paneled in mahogany or because of the long oval table with the many leather chairs surrounding it. Sam quickly sized up the occupants as he walked slowly toward one of the empty chairs, before he was introduced. The tall man who sat stiffly in his chair and stared straight ahead obviously was Colonel Albert Thurman. Although he was dressed in a conservative blue business suit, he wore it like a uniform. The blond woman with the closely cropped hair nervously twisting her wedding ring on her finger was undoubtedly the Colonel's wife, Althea. Her head was bowed slightly, leaving the impression of many years' submissiveness to a domineering husband. She wore a jumper with a blouse buttoned high under her chin. Her shoulders were rounded, and she was much younger than her husband. On the other side of the Colonel sat Howard Dredge, who appeared as old as the firm he represented, although Sam knew they both were about the same age. Part of this illusion was created by the pince-nez glasses he affected. The middle-aged angular woman next to Dredge was his secretary. Her shorthand book was open on the table in front of her. Raquel Thurman sat about three chairs away from the secretary.

"I don't really approve of this sort of approach," Dredge said ponderously. "However, I am willing to go along with my client's desires in the hopes that it will clarify any questions that might arise later and subsequently delay the administration of the estate." He opened his briefcase as he talked, and removed some legal documents.

"We're willing to cooperate in any way, Howard, so long as it does not jeopardize the interests of my client," Sam said. "What is it you have in mind?"

Dredge cleared his throat, removed his glasses, and pinched the bridge of his nose with thumb and forefinger. "Colonel Thurman fully realizes that Miss Raquel Thurman has no legal claim upon the estate of the late Cyrus Thurman, Sr., but he is prepared to make a settlement to avoid any acrimonious litigation."

Sam glanced toward Trudy, whose ball-point pen was flicking across the lines of her open notebook. "What kind of settlement did you have in mind, Howard?" he asked mildly.

"A very generous one indeed. We are prepared to go as high as twenty percent of the entire estate."

Raquel raised her eyebrows and slowly began to rock back and forth in her chair. "Do you have an idea of the value of the estate?" Sam asked.

"We have an approximation only. It is slightly in excess of three million dollars, and that includes the value of the property in Mexico."

Sam nodded. "I took a loose figure of one hundred and fifty thousand for the value of the Mexican holdings." He tipped back in his chair, clasped his hands in back of his head, and rested an ankle on his knee. "I would agree with you that it would be a good idea to settle this thing amicably, and I will so recommend to Miss Thurman, but not on the terms you suggest."

"What terms do you suggest?"

"An even division, which I am sure would be as Cy wanted it, and, of course, Miss Thurman will be the administratrix."

The Colonel stiffened and opened his mouth, then closed it when Dredge placed his hand on his forearm. "There is no way she can become administratrix, Sam. She is not one of the legal heirs. This perhaps is unfortunate from her point of view, but from a legal point of view there is no question, as you know."

"No, I don't know."

"Surely you have seen a copy of the will."

"Yes."

"Then you know that the late Cyrus Thurman clearly excluded her as a beneficiary when he designated that the heir be a product of his body. The will is dated after the birth of Cyrus Thurman, Jr. There is no confusion over intent."

"I believe he said the heirs of his body, not the heir."

"A reference, in case he had some other natural heir. I don't think there is any dispute, and there is nothing personal intended in this, that your client is the result of an artificial insemination." He put his glasses back on.

"The intent of my father was obvious and reasonable," the Colonel suddenly snapped. "There is nothing of the family in his two other alleged heirs. One was nothing but a damned hippie."

"And the other?" Raquel said, deadly sweet.

Again Dredge placed his hand on his client's arm.

"And Junior was a damned fine artist," Raquel added. "Some of his paintings were sold at an excellent price. One of them—"

"Excuse me, Miss Thurman," Sam said mildly, holding up his hand. She shrugged and turned her chair so that its back was facing the Colonel. The Colonel's face had gone blank. His wife still concentrated on the wedding ring she turned around on her finger. "Do you have any objection to Miss Thurman being appointed administratrix?" he asked.

Howard Dredge sighed and shook his head. "In view of the circumstances, I think our offer is most generous," he said, placing his papers back in his briefcase. "Can we expect your cooperation in determining the assets of the estate?"

"I think the first step is to have the probate judge determine the matter of who is to be the administratrix," Sam said. "If Colonel Thurman is appointed, of course we shall cooperate."

Dredge nodded. "I will see if I can get it set down for a quick hearing," he said.

"I have already done this," Sam replied in the same mild tone. "It's set for ten A.M. the day after tomorrow. If you want a continuance, I have no objection, however."

The Colonel pushed his chair back angrily and stood up. "While you loot the estate?" he shouted. "There will be no goddamn continuance." He turned toward his wife. "Put on your coat," he commanded.

Dredge suddenly held up his hand, and the Colonel paused. "Am I correct in assuming that a will has been filed for probate?" he asked with a puzzled expression on his face.

Sam nodded benignly. "Earlier this afternoon," he replied.

"The original?"

Again Sam nodded. "The late Cyrus Thurman had brought it with him, and it was found in his personal effects."

"What else was in his personal effects?"

"Shorts, socks, dressing kit, and shirts," Sam said. "The usual sort of thing a man takes for a short trip."

Dredge pulled his lips into a thin straight line as he stood up. Althea slipped into her coat and began buttoning it from the neck down. Just the trace of a faint smile played around her lips. A moment later they all left the room, without another comment.

When the door shut, Raquel turned in her chair, her mouth creased in a wide smile. "You were magnificent," she said elatedly. "I don't know what you did, but you were absolutely magnificent." She jumped from her chair, came toward him, and for an instant Sam thought she was going to kiss him. Instead she went to Trudy and looked over her shoulder. "Now, how do you write 'goddamn' in shorthand?" she asked.

Trudy smiled and pointed to a line of curlicues with her pen. Raquel looked at them curiously for a moment, then turned toward him. "Will you buy me a drink?"

He looked at his watch. It was a little after five. "Why not?" he said.

Lars Burton put down the telephone and went out to his car. Saxeby was behaving erratically again. He had left the print shop a little later than was his habit, and presently was in a small bar on Turk Street. On three occasions he had made a call from the public telephone in the bar, but the calls had not been completed. The last time he had banged the phone so hard in the cradle that the bartender had requested that he take it easy.

Burton was beginning to think of Saxeby as a person rather than merely as another suspect. The man had no friends, nor did he seek any. Any overtures from his fellow workers were rebuffed. He was one of the easiest men to keep under surveillance, because nothing seemed to attract his attention. When he walked through the supermarket after picking up his nightly six-pack of beer, he shouldered people aside with as much subtlety as a football player. Yet it was not an aggressive trait in his character. When he drove, he never appeared to become angry if someone cut in front of him. On the other hand, when he wished to change a lane in traffic, he did so with no regard to an oncoming car, nor did he pay any attention to an enraged blast of a horn when he cut someone off. He was oblivious of everything but himself.

The bar was sleazy. Its entertainment came from a television set angled high in one corner of the room. Its patrons were all male, except for two probable prostitutes who sat silently at a round table in the middle of the room. The detective bellied up to the bar, belched quietly, and ordered a draft beer. From the corner of his eye he spotted Saxeby sitting at the curve in the counter. He was concentrating on the foam in his beer glass. A man at the other end of the bar finished his beer and left. Burton recognized him as one of the men assigned to the trail car.

Burton took a preliminary sip from his beer, then drifted over to the telephone hanging on the wall by the street entrance. He called headquarters, his back to the bar, read the telephone number from the circular disk in the center of the dial, and ordered an intercept. When he turned around, Saxeby was standing directly behind him, not looking at him, concentrating instead on the telephone.

The detective went back to his seat. He heard two bells from the dime falling in its slot, and a moment later a third bell as another nickel was added to the coin box. A moment later the receiver once again crashed into its cradle. The bartender looked over. Saxeby walked back to the bar. His feet squished on the tile, and Burton, turning on his stool, saw that the man wore ripple-soled shoes. He saw also that there was something heavy in Saxeby's right-hand jacket pocket, something large enough to be a gun.

Saxeby paid for his beer and left the bar. "Looks like he is mad at someone," Burton said to the bartender.

The bartender nodded. "Yeah."

"Do you get many like him?"

The bartender looked at him closer. His eyes narrowed, and Burton knew he had been pegged as a cop once again. Corona could run around with a badge pinned to his lapel and no one ever recognized him as a cop. All Burton had to do was open his mouth. "Never seen him before, sir," the bartender said. "Never been in here when I'm on shift." He moved away.

Burton went back to his car, which he had parked in a loading zone. He could have Saxeby picked up on a traffic violation, and they probably would get him on a concealed-weapons charge. But they would have nothing more than that.

The radio came on his frequency. "He's crossed Market Street to Mission Street." Burton sat in his car, unrolled an antacid tablet, and popped it in his mouth. "Subject has entered the tiered garage near the *Chronicle*," the radio said.

He was going to turn himself in to a newspaper. Burton smiled wryly. It was strange a man who had a reason not to talk would absolutely refuse to unless some newsman pushed a microphone in front of him, or he knew that what he said would appear in the paper, and a million or so people could either hear it or read it. He turned the thought over in his mind as the detail tagging Saxeby reported at short intervals. The suspect was out of the garage and had entered the Chronicle Building.

Burton slid the car into gear and slowly drove toward the Chronicle Building. Saxeby's visit had been brief, and he had just come out of the newspaper building as Burton arrived. The detective waited until the detail reported that Saxeby had reentered the garage, and then went into the newspaper building and showed his badge to the guard.

"He came to pick up some picture for a Miss Thurman," the guard said. "A copy boy brought it down."

It took a little while to find the copy boy, but when he was located, he took Burton to the photo lab. The night crew did not know

122

much about it. The picture had been ordered and printed by the day side, but according to the order, it had been ordered by Raquel Thurman, and it was a "mug shot" of her. They found the original print in the files. It had been taken the day after the murder of her father, when a reporter and photographer had interviewed her at her home.

"She's a good-looking broad," one of the photographers said.

Lars agreed that she was indeed. A reporter came into the room, and the detective recognized him as Doug Kennedy. "It's just a way-out lead," the detective said. "How was it ordered?"

The reporter looked at the carbon order form. "It says cash. Someone either came in, or the order was mailed in."

"Can you check?"

"Not tonight. Can do first thing in the morning."

"If it was a letter, will you save it for us?"

"Sure. But why don't you ask the Thurman woman?"

Lars sighed. "We've got a suspect, that's all. If you print it, you'll burn the whole bit."

"We always cooperate," the reporter said. "Who's the suspect?"

"If you call Gus Corona, he can probably tell you more about it."

The reporter grinned. "From what I hear, I can talk to the Thurman woman at the same time. Local cop has thing with heiress."

Burton looked at him blankly, belched, and reached for his antacid tablets. "There's no way we can check to see if there is a letter now?"

Kennedy shook his head. "The business office doesn't open until tomorrow at nine. If there was a letter, they may not have kept it."

"Well, see what you can do."

He left the building and returned to his car. The evening

traffic crush was easing. A wino walking with exaggerated care came toward him. He stopped when he was parallel with the police car, then moved over, stuck his head in the window, and asked for a quarter. Burton gave it to him, but when the man wanted to become friendly, he told him to move on, and turned up the volume on the radio. There was nothing on the frequency but static. He waited for about five minutes before he picked up the microphone and called the trail car.

"He's still in the garage," the radio responded.

Burton looked at his watch. "He came out of the building three-quarters of an hour ago."

"Yeah. We saw him go in, but he hasn't come out yet."

"Is there an exit on Minna Street?"

There was a long silence. "I guess there is," the voice said uncertainly.

Burton sighed and drove around to the back side of the garage. There was indeed an exit on Minna Street. The gate attendant did not remember a car departing that answered the description of Saxeby's, but a thorough search of the garage failed to turn it up inside.

A half-hour later Lars Burton issued an all-points bulletin to locate, but not pick up, the car. Another undercover car was dispatched to Saxeby's house, but two hours after Saxeby had left the newspaper building, he had not returned to his home.

Sam Benedict felt more like he was on a date than with a client. Raquel Thurman demanded attention, and she got it. When she walked down the street, she was a menace to traffic, both pedestrian and automotive. Males bumped into each other, their eyes fastened on her as she passed. Cars slowed. A uniformed cop made a low wolf call with his traffic whistle when they crossed the street. It had been particularly noticeable in the financial district along Montgomery Street when they had left his office. On the roof of the Mark

Hopkins Hotel, he had taken a table near a window, and most of the male patrons at the bar had slid down to one end, where they could get the best view.

Now it was a little better. They were at the Trianon, and she was getting some competition from other women who had arrived with their escorts for an early dinner before the evening show at the Geary Theater. They had both been here before and both knew Jimmy Collette, the owner and maître d'.

She ordered the wild boar, and Sam did also. "I really don't know why they call it wild boar when they are grown on his own ranch in Marin County somewhere," she commented.

"They are captive wild boar," Sam said.

"They can't be wild if they are captive."

"Think of it as a polar bear in the zoo," Sam said. "If he served polar-bear steaks, from polar bears that he raised, they still would be wild polar-bear steaks." She laughed. "Never argue with a lawyer. You know what my father once said? He said that we must always be kind to lawyers and remember that they once were little children too."

"He was quoting Charles Lamb."

"From boars to lambs in thirty seconds. And bores remind me of Albert and Althea. His mother tells me that Albert is somewhat of a spendthrift."

"Albert?" A quizzical expression flickered across her face. "In some ways he is, and in some ways he isn't. Dad once told me that when he was a kid, Albert used to get ten dollars a week allowance. Then around every Wednesday or Thursday, he would go to Stella and bum another dollar or two, saying he was broke. Then one day Dad went into Albert's room and found him counting his loot. He had a tackle box full of it, more than eight hundred dollars in all. A few weeks later, Dad said, he 'invested' it and lost it all, but I never did find out what the investment was. I never asked. He bought a cruiser, which he keeps at the Golden Gate Yacht Club, but all he does is talk about it. He never uses it. He named it the *Excelsior*. So in one way he is penurious, and in another way he is a spendthrift."

"How long has he been in the Army?"

"Forever. He's a professional. I suppose it is because if Althea ever rebelled and stole away with his little security blanket, he would still have another through the Army. Not that she ever will."

"Is she rich?"

"Is she? She's a loaded little brown wren. She got it from her mother, who was an oil or cigarette heiress or something like that. That's why Albert married her. She even owns the house they live in."

"That's interesting."

"She lets Albert browbeat her in every manner, but one. She won't let him have any of her money. I think she pays the house bills and taxes and things like that, but the stern and stalwart Colonel probably doesn't get as much money out of her as he did out of Stella when he was a kid. I think she is pretty sharp in financial matters. That's probably why she had her grandfather write up the will in the manner it was."

Sam raised his eyebrows. "She knew about the artificial insemination?"

"We all knew about it. Dad told us when we were kids, but, as he said, it was no big deal, because we were still his kids. It was like an adoption, sort of, I guess. Dorothy—that's my mother—wanted to adopt a Hungarian girl, and Dad explained that she would be just as much a part of the family as we were."

"What happened to her?"

"The papers never went through, because Dorothy was killed in an automobile accident on the Bayshore Freeway."

The waiter removed their plates, and Sam ordered two Stregas. "Any more problems in Sausalito?" he asked presently.

126

"No. Gus is living there," she replied casually. And then: "I bet you spent my retainer on the drinks and the dinner tonight."

He smiled. "Just about. I'm keeping a record of the expenses, and I'll have them on the bill I render after we win this case." He finished his liqueur. "Where are you parked?"

She grinned. "In Sausalito. I came in with Gus. He's working late."

"How are you going to get back?"

"If you don't take me, I might be able to find a cab," she replied, her eyes on the top of her glass.

Sam chuckled softly and signed the check. "I'd be delighted to take you home, young lady," he said.

They took a taxi to his house, where they transferred to his Mercedes. The night was crystal clear, and a cool breeze came in from the west off the ocean. The lights from the bridge hung like a pendant across the Golden Gate, as they skirted the edge of the Presidio and came up on the bridge approaches. "I think I must have a hundred color slides of the bridge," she said, "yet if I am alone and have my camera with me, I'll stop again and shoot a couple more, particularly when it is like this."

"Are you a photo buff?"

"Um-umph. It's a hobby. I can even develop my own color if its Ektachrome. There is a utility room below the house that I converted into a dark room." She paused and then said, "How much is twenty percent of three million?"

"Six hundred thousand."

"That's a lot of money."

"Do you want to take the settlement?"

"Of course not. I couldn't bear to think of the rest of the money just sitting in a bank somewhere."

"I expect to win the case," he replied, "but I should warn you that there is always the possibility of losing, and you will have nothing."

"Oh, hell. Let's go for broke." They turned off on the Sausalito road, and he saw the moon rising over the city. "Gus told me that the Astro is influenced by the full moon," she said.

"That one's a long way from being full."

She remained silent until they reached the center of the village, and then, although he knew the way, she told him to turn left and climb the hill. A few minutes later she pointed to the carport, and he drove a little past it and backed in beside her small sports car. Two small dots of green flashed in the beam of the headlights, the eyes of a small wild animal or a cat, and then disappeared. He turned off the lights, then got out of the car and opened the door on her side. "Would you care for a drink?" she asked, sliding out of the car.

Before he could answer, there was a sharp crack from above him on the hill, and a split second later something struck the car and then screamed off into the night with a vicious whine. He reacted with no conscious forethought. Pushing her violently back into the car, he threw himself on the floor of the carport, just as another shot was fired. The bullet thudded into the open car door, pushing it shut. She cried out as the bottom of the door slammed against her shins. "Pull in your legs," he whispered. He felt a faint surprise that he did not shout the order. At the same time, he wriggled along the floor to the back of the car; then, rising to a crouch, he worked his way to the left-hand door, inched it open, and slid in behind the wheel. The third shot went through the exact center of the windshield, creating an instantaneous maze of splintered glass around the small neat hole. Raquel huddled on the floor of the car, moaning softly. He reached across her to pull the door shut.

Another sharp crack split the still night. This time the bullet went through the radiator and splattered under the hood of the car. Sam swore softly, straightened, and turned the key in the ignition. The engine caught instantly, but with a continuous rasping screech. He knew that one of the blades was scratching against the radiator

128

core. The tires spun on the wooden platform of the carport, and the powerful car leaped out to the roadway. As he made the turn, the car dipped slightly, slithered into the shoulder, and then, as he straightened it out, the engine froze. He glanced over his shoulder and saw headlights flash on a car parked on the switchback of the road. Again Sam swore softly. He slipped the gears into neutral, and presently the car, at an agonizingly slow speed, began to coast down the steep hill toward the village far below. When he drifted into the first turn, he heard the tires of the car behind him shriek as it spun into the preceding curve. The beams of its headlights were ahead of him, sweeping over the side of his car as it came out of the turn. Instinctively he hunched over the wheel, then straightened, realizing that no man could drive and shoot a gun at this speed on this road.

Now the Mercedes began to gather speed, but the pursuing car had closed the gap. Its driver flicked his headlights on high beam, and Sam quickly slapped his rear view mirror at an angle to turn off the glare. He went into another turn, and the car behind bumped him lightly, then was forced to brake. A split second later he heard a horrible screech of metal being torn, but his speed was so great that he did not dare risk a quick glance over his shoulder. The glare of the pursuing headlights had disappeared, and suddenly Sam was racing past the intersection that turned off in front of the Alta Mira Hotel at the top of the incline before the traffic light at the bottom of the hill. The light was red, and two cars waited patiently in front of it. Jamming on the brakes, he locked the wheels, screeched past the two waiting cars, and came to a halt in the middle of the intersection. For a long moment he remained motionless behind the wheel, catching his breath. Horns began to blare, and he slowly became aware of a rising babble of voices.

A tall young man, bearded and with his hair caught in a pony tail, stepped off the sidewalk over to him, bent down, and peered in the window. "You okay, man?"

129

Sam exhaled slowly and nodded.

"Your chick don't look so good. I'll call an ambulance." The hippie ran from the car.

Sam looked at Raquel. She lay with her head on the floor, one leg up on the seat. Her mouth was open, and her eyes were closed.

11

*S*HORTLY AFTER MIDNIGHT, Gus
Corona arrived at Sam's apartment carrying an early edition of the
morning paper, which bannered the story:

SAM BENEDICT, HEIRESS
ESCAPE SNIPER ATTACK

The attorney read no more than the headline before he
smiled wryly and motioned for Corona to help himself to a drink.
"We put your girl friend in a private hospital for the night. She's
suffering from a mild shock, but they say she will be all right in the
morning."

"Yeah, I know."

"If she's agreeable, I think I'll move her in here. I'll have Trudy move in, too. The security is a little better here."

Gus Corona nodded, walked over to the bar, and poured himself a Scotch and water. Sam Benedict certainly had not been very shaken up, he thought. The attorney looked as if he had just returned from a country club, with his alpaca sweater, soft flannel pants, and moccasin-type shoes. "There's a small restaurant called the Caprice out in Tiburon just beyond Sausalito. It's on the water, and most of its customers park across the street. A couple named Kevin reported their brand new Olds was stolen while they were in the restaurant. He's a rancher from eastern Oregon and is used to leaving his keys in the car. They are staying at the Alta Mira. About an hour ago a California Highway Patrol car found the Kevin car parked in almost the same spot from where it had been stolen, only one side had been bashed in pretty badly. There was a rifle shell on the floor of the front seat."

"How did he get through the intersection?"

Gus sipped from his drink. "He apparently turned left in front of the Alta Mira Hotel and came out farther down the road. Are you familiar with the Alta Mira?"

"Yes."

"Well, you know they have an outside deck where they serve cocktails. There were several people there who heard the shots and the crash when the car sideswiped the hillside. Several of the more curious types went to the edge of the deck and tried to see what was going on. They saw your car go racing by. A moment later an Oldsmobile similar to the Kevin car made the turn in front of the hotel." He took another sip from his drink. "That's not all. A few yards behind the Olds was a black beat-up sedan with gull-like taillights. Saxeby drives a 1960 Ford with gull-like taillights."

"But you have Saxeby under surveillance."

The detective sighed. "Not for the past several hours," he replied, then told him about Saxeby's disappearance.

Sam Benedict sprawled lower in his chair and clasped his hands behind his head. "It doesn't make sense, Gus," he said presently. "The car that hit the bluff was the one that tried to run me off the road."

"And if Saxeby is the Astro, he has switched his pattern. He switched from killing at random on the appearance of a full moon to a vendetta toward one particular family."

Sam nodded. "That's what I mean. It doesn't make sense."

"I know what you are getting at," Corona replied. "The only one with any logical motive is the Colonel. But if we don't have enough evidence to pick up Saxeby, who is a bum, how in the hell can we pick up a Colonel in the United States Army? We can't even tail him. Can you imagine an undercover car going unnoticed very long inside the Presidio? Besides, even though he is a prick, it is unlikely that he was the one trying to lay you out tonight."

"Why?"

"This guy was in his car shooting at you from a little more than one hundred and fifty yards away, yet he missed you on four out of four shots. He was using a rifle."

Sam shook his head. "I've known some colonels who have never fired anything more than a command to their orderly. Have you got anything on him at all?"

"An item in a news column that he slapped his wife a couple of times in the Crown Room at the Fairmont. The columnist doesn't mention his name, but the librarian filed it under 'Albert Thurman.' It happened about two years ago." He paused. "I agree with you that it is unlikely that Saxeby would take some potshots at you."

"Why?"

"He'll need you to defend him."

Sam Benedict chuckled. "The sonofabitch will have to pay for my car first," he replied. "What are you going to do now?"

"Put a policewoman in Raquel's apartment for a few days as a decoy. Give her a long black wig and have her walk around. Sausalito is going to stake out the area for a few days."

"Didn't anyone see the Kevin car when it was parked up there?"

Gus nodded. "There was one complaint, no I.D. A woman said there was some hippie shooting off a gun. In that area, it's always a hippie."

At one thirty A.M. a prowl car found Saxeby's old Ford. It was moving slowly up Geary, and the driver was overcontrolling with the exaggerated caution of a drunk. Lars Burton, who was preparing to go home, was notified at headquarters. He sighed, looked at his watch, and thought that he now would have several more hours accumulated in overtime that he would be most unlikely to collect. He did not wait, however, to ponder his misfortune. Instead, he immediately called Communications and ordered that he be patched through to the prowl car that had spotted Saxeby. "Pick him up and bring him in," he said. "Use caution in approaching him, as he may be armed. Treat him like a gentleman if he comes easy, but tell him he's a suspect in a holdup."

He next called the front desk. "Any recent Caucasian hold-ups recently?"

"A drugstore on Sutter Street about an hour ago."

"That'll do." He belched. "They'll be bringing a drunk in named Saxeby. Don't book him, but take his effects from him and put him by himself in a holding room. Give him coffee if he wants it. Don't send out a wrecker to pick up his car. Just have it parked and locked at the curb where they take him."

Three-quarters of an hour later a uniformed man came into Burton's small office. Saxeby had offered no resistance and was high enough to spend the night in the drunk tank, but he had sobered up some when they told him he was a suspect in an armed robbery. His license had expired and showed a Culver City address. "He's spooky, though. He's very spooky," the cop added. "He hasn't said a word. He didn't even deny the holdup."

"Anything in the car?"

"Not a thing except dirt. There were used paper coffeecups, a couple of empty beer cans, a brown envelope from the *Chronicle* with a picture of some broad in it, a copy of today's paper with the Sam Benedict bit, a flashlight, and a current edition of a magazine called *Horoscope*."

Burton nodded and went out to the desk, where he asked for and was given a large envelope containing Saxeby's personal possessions. His wallet contained about fifty dollars; a key chain with four keys on it—a house key, a locker key, and two car keys; a small unopened coil of picture wire; and a faucet.

"I can't figure out what he was doing with a faucet," the sergeant said.

"Maybe he had a leak," Lars replied, taking the keys and passing the envelope back. "In a little while go in and give him the sweet treatment. Tell him that his car answers the description and that we are bringing the victim down for a lineup."

With the sparse morning traffic, Lars Burton was able to get out to the Sunset District in less than a half-hour. He parked a block away from Saxeby's row house, then walked briskly to the small dwelling, went up the stairs, and inserted the key in the lock. The house was smaller than an average apartment. The door opened into a tiny foyer. On the left was a small living room that contained no furniture at all. To the right was a small kitchen that smelled of onions and old chili. More than a dozen unwashed aluminum trays were piled on the counter. A frying pan was on the stove with yellow strips of old scrambled eggs stuck to its side. In the refrigerator were an unopened package of bacon, a half-dozen eggs, and two cans of beer. The closets were empty, except for one which held a few pots and pans and some kitchen hardware.

One of the bedrooms was unfurnished. Saxeby lived in the other. A television set was in one corner, with a remote control running to the nightstand next to the single bed. This room was as filthy as the kitchen. Another aluminum tray, from the prepared dinners, rested on top of a pile of magazines, all dealing with astrology. The bed was unmade, and the sheets were gray. Two well-worn suits hung in the closet. Two pairs of shoes lay on the floor, one with ripple soles, the other black leather wingtips with metal cleats in the heels. There was a two-drawer dresser. The bottom one was half-full of papers. He lifted them gently. Most appeared to be astrological charts. They reminded him of the work of some young student trying to solve a geometric problem. The top drawer contained some socks and shorts, professionally laundered, a half-dozen sport shirts, and a pair of silk pajamas with a high button collar. Lifting up the pajamas, he found a box of thirty-two-caliber bullets. He left them, stepped over the rubbish, and went out into the tiny hall.

A bathroom separated the two bedrooms. A steady stream came out of the hot-water faucet, and when he turned it, he found that it would not shut off. There was another valve below the basin, and this one worked. He shrugged. The bathroom was as dirty as the bedroom, the towels gray, the mirror so covered with dirt that his reflection was a blur, except for a small spot in the middle that had been rubbed clean. He opened the cabinet behind the mirror. It contained a shaving mug and brush, a safety razor, and a tube of used lipstick. Pale pink grease protruded from the bottom part of the tube. He picked it up carefully. It bore no brand name. The top of the tube rested next to it, and this bore initials in script, *CR*. He replaced them in the same position he had found them, and went back to the hall. To his right, at the end of the tiny corridor, was another door. He turned the knob and pulled, but the door refused to open. He looked at it more closely, then pursed his lips. It had been nailed shut with huge spikes at the top, the jamb and the bottom. He checked the walls of the bedroom and the living room. The door did not open into a closet. It would be too deep to be a closet and too small to be another room. Then it occurred to him that it probably opened on stairs leading to the garage below.

He glanced at his watch. Saxeby now had been in the holding room for an hour, the detective calculated. He went through the house, shutting off the lights. A moment later he went out the front door, testing it to make sure that it was locked, then went down the steps to the garage. There was no lock or hasp on the overhanging door, not even a hand grip with which it could be raised. He kicked it tentatively at the base to see if there was any give. There was. The door was not nailed. It occurred to him that it might be electronically operated, and he began searching for a photoelectric cell.

The lights suddenly went on in the house next door. A window flew up, and a fat old witch with hair askew pushed out her head. "What in hell are you doing out there?" she screamed. "It's three o'clock in the morning."

Lars Burton suddenly slouched. "I'm looking for my friend," he said, his words heavily slurred. "Are you my ole friend?"

"Go on, beat it, you goddamn wino. I'm goin' to call the cops. Can't never get no goddamn sleep." The window banged down.

Burton belched; and then, weaving slightly, he crossed the street and headed toward his car. When he turned the corner, he straightened and walked briskly up the street. When he turned the next corner, a prowl car suddenly appeared around the corner and presently drew up beside him. "You lost, buddy?"

"I'm Burton of Homicide."

"Now I've heard them all," the cop said, getting out of the car.

Burton started to reach for his wallet.

The cop had his gun out as quickly as a western movie marshal. "Put your hands up in the air, please," he said. "Then walk over to the car, bend over, and put your hands way out on the hood."

The detective did as he was instructed. "Right-hand-rear pocket," he said as the cop professionally ran his hands over his body. A moment later he felt a gentle tug as his wallet was removed and opened to his badge.

"Sorry, sir," the cop said. "We had a report of a prowler."

"You were pretty fast."

"We were in the neighborhood."

"I wish there had been a prowl car in another neighborhood earlier tonight," Burton said, folding his wallet back into his pocket. "Would have saved us a lot of work. Where did your report come from?"

"On 46th Street in the 1900 block headed this way. Was that you?"

Burton nodded. "Yeah, it was me. It might be a good idea to drive up and down the block and flash your lights around."

"Will do." The cop grinned and went back to his car.

A half-hour later Burton gave the keys back to the desk sergeant and watched him replace them in the envelope. "How is our pigeon?"

"He's pretty sober. He says he was pub crawling and that he knew he was going to get picked up because of some garbage about Mercury going backward."

"Have someone tell him they picked up the suspect in Oakland and that he can go. Be apologetic and take him back to his car and tell him you will have someone follow him home so he won't get picked up again. Let me know if he drives his car into his garage or leaves it in the driveway."

Then he went to his office and began typing out another report to be added to the burgeoning file on Raymond Saxeby. Before he was finished, he received a telephone report from the cop that had followed Saxeby home.

The suspect had parked in the driveway, taken his flashlight from the steering post of his car, and paying no attention to the prowl car outside, had run the beam up and down the hinged side of the door at the top of the steps. Then he had directed the beam along the floor of the small porch, picked something up, and gone inside.

Lars Burton sighed. It was the old match trick, where a paper match or a piece of paper was placed in a doorjamb. Whenever who set it up returned, and found it gone, it meant that someone had opened the door during his absence. It was so old that Burton had never thought of it. It meant also that Saxeby was smarter than was thought. No, not smart, but cunning. Now Saxeby would be more alert, and it would be much more difficult to keep him under surveillance.

The detective wrote all of this in his report, along with a request for a search warrant for the Saxeby premises, and sent a carbon copy by interdepartmental mail to Gus Corona.

12

─────────

*I*T WAS A LITTLE after nine thirty when Sam Benedict entered his office, closely followed by Trudy, and sat down in his high-backed leather chair behind his massive desk. She placed two piles of pink telephone-message slips in front of him. "The big file is from the media," she said disapprovingly. "All wanting some comment on your peccadilloes last night."

"It's not an accurate description," he said mildly, wondering why she appeared more annoyed than concerned.

Trudy ignored his criticism. "Mrs. Baumgartner has canceled her eleven-o'clock appointment. Her husband bought her a new car, and she is sufficiently impressed to put off the divorce again."

"This about the third time, isn't it?"

"The fourth. Inspector Corona has called twice. Miss Raquel Thurman called from Winston Hospital to say she has accepted your offer to have her move in."

"Did you bring your suitcase?"

"I wasn't asked."

"The suggestion wasn't made to Miss Thurman until shortly before midnight. I decided that the notification of your role as a chaperon could wait until this morning." He smiled. "Have I ever told you the story of the lawyer-client relationship?"

"Many times, Sam. You know as well as I do that this woman could turn on a eunuch. Without me around, she could have you in bed after the first Scotch, if she wanted to."

His smile broadened. "You know, I am surprised that you would think of me as a eunuch."

Her lip trembled. "We both know better than that. What I think is unfair is that you didn't tell me about last night. I had to read about it in the newspapers. Why do you get so involved?"

"I had no intention of carrying it to that extreme, and I would be willing to testify to this under oath."

The trembling lip turned into the start of a smile. "It's not that I worry about you," she said. "It's just that it plays hell with my job security." She bent across the desk to pick up the stack of media messages, and he caught the faint odor of her perfume. "You can't possibly answer all of these," she said. "We can set up a press conference in place of the Baumgartner appointment. Shall I have a bar set up in the board room?"

He nodded. "Be sure to tell them, however, that it is extremely unlikely that I can give them anything new."

She turned and walked across the room toward the door. She wore a gold-colored link belt around her waist, and a large key that hung from the end of the belt swung in unison with the sway of her hips. She wore a blue knit suit that clung to every curve. Her body did not have the ripe lushness of Raquel's, but it would look good a lot longer. She paused by the door and looked back over her shoulder, and now she was smiling. "I brought my suitcase," she said, "and a garment bag."

He laughed as she went out of the room. Then he picked up the telephone and called Corona.

Bill Bell was an old man. Almost fifteen years ago he had retired at the age of sixty-five as a longshoreman, but rarely a day passed that he did not go down to the docks along the waterfront to watch the ships being loaded and unloaded and to reminisce with anyone who would spare the time about the old days when the union was constantly fighting the capitalists. Today there was no one to talk to, and when he noticed a ship slowly moving past Alcatraz Island, he hobbled out to the end of the pier for a closer look. It was a big one flying the flag of Japan, and it carried the new mechanical booms over its hatches that the capitalists had invented to put longshoremen out of work. He leaned over the edge of the pier and spit his disgust into the water. It was then that he saw the body. It bumped gently against one of the pilings. It was lying face down in the water, and it was encased in a gray sweater and gray pants. There were no shoes on the feet, and the yellow hair around the head was either close-cropped for a woman or long for a man. Another thing that made it difficult to tell the sex was because it had been in the water for a long time. The corpse was bloated, and swelled against the clothes. He watched it for a few moments, then remembered that he should probably tell the police. If he did not, the union-busting lackeys of the capitalists would probably come around and crack his skull open, and he was getting too old for that. He turned and hobbled back down the pier.

A few moments before the press conference ended, one of the

secretaries came in and gave Trudy a note. Trudy waited until the last of the television crews had finished their cutaway shots, then walked over to Sam and told him that he was late for his twelve-o'clock appointment. He knew that he had no noon appointment, but he looked at his watch and commented that he was surprised that the time had gone so quickly. "Have another drink," he said, waving his arm to all of them. Following Trudy, he left the board room and went out into the reception room. One reporter came after him, Doug Kennedy of the *Chronicle*.

"Yesterday someone came in and bought a picture we ran of Raquel Thurman," Kennedy said quickly. "Do you have any comment on this?"

"Who did?"

"A guy with close-cropped white hair, wearing a sport shirt and pants. Are you aware of this?"

Sam looked at his watch. "Maybe it is one of these writers for a fact detective magazine. Don't they always collect pictures of the principals?"

"Not when the cops are tailing him," Kennedy said. "And whenever Sam Benedict answers a question with a question, he is just like every other lawyer. He's trying to hide something."

Sam laughed and held out his hands. "You're too good a reporter, Doug," he replied. "And I can tell you this truthfully. I didn't know anything about this, but I am going to try to find out."

"The detective who was asking about it is Lars Burton of Homicide, and he's the one who has been working almost full time on the Astro. Is this what you had in mind when you said a few minutes ago that the case would break in the near future?"

"I didn't know about this. I think the case will break because the pressures are getting so great on whoever killed the Thurmans, at least, that the whole business will cave in. As I said earlier, what happened last night is a strong indication of this."

"When you say 'at least,' you mean you don't think the Astro is to blame?"

"At this point I have no idea who killed the Thurmans or who set me up last night. I have theories only, and you couldn't print them if I told them to you."

The reporter grinned and stuck out his hand. "Okay," he said, "but I'll keep bugging you, just like the Astro may be getting bugged because someone is muscling, in on his act."

Sam chuckled, shook hands, then went back to his private office. A moment later Trudy slipped into the door behind him and placed a piece of paper with a typewritten address on it in front of him. "Gus Corona called back during the conference," she said. "The reason you couldn't get him was because he was heading for that address with a young female named Amelia Jones. It seems that Amelia is very reluctant to talk to him without a lawyer present, preferably you. I told him that you probably would be there by twelve thirty."

Amelia Jones was thin to the point of emaciation. When Sam first saw her sitting in the police car, she appeared as a child barely in her teens, but when she. got out, he revised his estimate up to the mid-twenties. She was barefoot. Her breasts were no more than buds, and her hips were boyishly thin. Her hair was a light reddish brown and hung down to her waist.

"Our little friend here does not trust the fuzz," Gus Corona said, leaning against the side of the police car. "However, if there is someone present who is an attorney like Sam Benedict who will protect her rights, she is willing to let us into the apartment of Cyrus Thurman, Jr., and one in which she also has been living for the past two or three weeks."

Sam glanced toward the detective, who winked broadly. He sensed that Corona was angry, but there was nothing other than his sarcasm to indicate it.

144

"How do I know it's him?" she asked in an extraordinarily high soprano voice.

Sam took out his wallet, extracted his driver's license, and showed it to the girl, who carefully studied the picture on it before she passed it back.

"You want me to go buy you a paper?" Corona asked. "His picture is all over that."

"I don't read the papers much," the girl said. "You can't believe them."

Corona pushed himself away from the car. "Let's go to the apartment," he said.

"Is it okay?" the girl asked.

Sam nodded. "It's okay," he said.

It was a five-story building off North Beach, and the stairs had been built on the outside of the building. They walked up the five floors, the girl in front and Gus Corona in the rear. At the top was a small landing, and while Sam caught his breath, the girl removed a single key from her jeans, unlocked the door, and walked in ahead of them. It was a studio designed for an artist. More than half of the ceiling was a glass skylight. At one end of the room was a small dais on which there was a single folding chair. Around the walls were more than fifty canvases, some abstract, some nudes of an almost photographic reproduction. Several of them he recognized instantly as portraits of the girl standing beside him. An easel was in front of the dais. The only furniture in the room were three directors' chairs. Off to the right was a small bedroom and a bath. There was no kitchen. A brown sack dress hung over the foot of the bed.

The girl stepped up on the dais, sat down in the folding chair, and pulled her legs up in the full-lotus position. "So ask me questions," she said. The light from the skylight made her eyes an intense blue.

"You holding a class?" Gus Corona asked mildly.

The girl said nothing.

"We need your help," Sam replied, breaking a long silence. "You were a friend of Cy Thurman, Jr., and he was very close to his sister, whom I represent. Neither one of us is here to antagonize you. We think there is a possibility you may help us."

"Like I said, ask me questions." She adjusted her position slightly on the chair.

"Did you live here with Cy?"

"Sometimes. I did before, and I did later. In between there was Big Boobs, only she didn't live here. She was married, but she was chasing him around. He'd just sort of go along."

"Who is Big Boobs?"

She shook her head. "I don't know her name. She called Cy "Junior," but everyone else called him Cy. Once Cy said that he had known her a long time and that she had problems. She sure did have problems."

"What kind of problems?"

The girl leaned forward, and her long hair fell over her shoulders. "Like sex, mostly. At first she used to pose for him up here, but then when he told her about the Art Barn, she'd rather go down there."

"How do you know she had sex problems?"

The girl sighed. "She'd get her gun off the minute she'd get out of her clothes. The more that were around, the more it would go off. She was a weirdo."

"Was Junior having an affair with her?"

She tipped her head. "You mean, like, did he ball her?"

"If you put it that way, yes."

"I guess." She paused. "I never saw him. The guru at the Art Barn was."

Sam settled back in his director's chair. "Would you recognize her if you saw her again?"

"I don't know. I never paid too much attention to her, because she was all uptight, and I didn't like her too much."

"When did you last see her?"

"About a month ago. The day Cy was beaten up was the last time I saw her. She never came back in here. I brought Cy back up here and took care of him. He had a black eye and a bloody nose, and one of his teeth was loose. I brought Cy back up here and fixed him up. He told me then that we'd probably never see Big Boobs again."

"Tell me about him getting beaten up."

"I wasn't there."

"Did he talk about it?"

"Not much. I remember he said everyone talked about us being hung-up, but it was really the older generation who had the hang-up scene. I was in the Art Barn that afternoon when Big Boobs was gunning around. I left for a while, and when I came back, Cy and Big Boobs were just leaving."

"Did he always take her back and forth?"

"Yeah. Once I heard the guru ask him why he bothered, and he explained that she had problems and that this probably was helping her over her hang-up."

"What car did he get in that night?"

"It wasn't night. It was late afternoon. She always came in the daytime, except once, when she was late leaving because she was a little high on grass. He used the psychedelic bus."

"And it was when he came back from this trip that he had been beaten up."

"He wasn't on any trip. He didn't even smoke pot."

Sam resisted a smile. "Forgive me. After he returned from taking this woman home, he was beaten up."

"That's right."

"And he didn't say who had assaulted him?"

"All he said was that we probably wouldn't be seeing Big

147

Boobs again, so I figured it was her husband, but he didn't say, and I didn't ask him."

"Did he paint many pictures of this woman?"

"Yeah, a lot."

"What happened to them?"

The girl pulled her hair from her eyes with both hands.

"What happened to them?" Sam prompted.

"I threw them away."

"Where?"

"In the trash."

Gus Corona stood up and slowly began to walk around the room, then paused in front of one nude of Amelia Jones. She was in much the same position as she was now, except that her hands were crossed between her legs.

"What happened to those in the Art Barn?"

"There was only one of Big Boobs there. Some guy came in and bought it."

"Before or after Junior was assaulted?"

"I don't remember. The guru would know."

"How long had Junior lived here?"

"A long time. Before I met him."

Corona drifted into the bedroom, glanced around, then came back out.

"And all the pictures of this Big Boobs have disappeared?"

The girl hesitated, then nodded.

"If we could get one, it might help us solve his murder."

"Once you're dead, you're dead."

"It possibly could save someone else from becoming dead."

Amelia Jones uncoiled her legs, put both feet on the floor, and presently one began to go up and down rapidly. After a while Sam took out his wallet and extracted a one-hundred-dollar bill. Then he stood up, walked over to her, and pressed the bill into her hands.

"Please," he said quietly. "It is very important. They tried to kill Junior's sister last night."

She wet her lips. "He gave one to a friend," she said slowly. "I'll have to find him."

"Okay, let's go find him now," Corona said.

"I'd have to ask around." She shook her head as she spoke.

Sam gestured toward the detective. "How long will it take to find this friend?"

"I think he works. I'll have to ask around."

Sam took out a pen and a card and scribbled his home address on it. "If you can get it tonight, bring it to this address," he said quietly. "If it's tomorrow, bring it to the office address. Either place, you'll get another hundred dollars when you bring it."

Amelia Jones suddenly looked down at the bill in her hand, and her eyes widened. "Wow," she said softly. "I've never seen one of these before."

Gus Corona brought Raquel to the penthouse late in the afternoon. She looked none the worse for her experience, although her manner was more subdued. Earlier the detective had gone to her home in Sausalito. With the help of the policewoman there he had packed three suitcases, causing her to comment wryly that she was not planning a permanent move. Nevertheless, according to Trudy, who had shown her to her room, she had unpacked everything and presently was taking a shower.

She emerged about three-quarters of an hour later wearing a belted hostess gown, with obviously nothing on underneath it, and a pair of gold sandals. All of the Thurmans were a little unconventional, Sam thought as he made her a drink and told her in capsule form of their interview with Amelia Jones.

"I doubt that she will show up," Corona predicted. "She's probably halfway to L.A. by now."

"It's strange how much more a person learns about someone

close to him after he's dead," Raquel said. "Junior told me he had a pad, but I had always imagined it to be a small room somewhere. I didn't know he really painted. I thought he was faggy, and he turns out to be a stud."

Sam waited until Gus Corona was well into his second drink before he mildly accused him of holding out on him.

"How?"

"Last night someone whom you have had under surveillance went to the *Chronicle* and bought a picture of Raquel. He wore a sport shirt. He has close-cropped hair, and he is suspected of being the Astro."

"There was so much going on, I forgot to tell you about the picture. We picked the guy up later on a robbery suspicion. Burton went through his house. The garage seems to be nailed shut. The house is dirty. A box of thirty-two-caliber bullets was in a drawer, but no gun. He had no gun on him when we rousted him."

Raquel walked slowly toward the sliding glass doors, and Sam watched her with more than passing interest. Trudy cleared her throat, and Sam resisted an impulse to look toward her. "What does he want with my picture?" Raquel asked.

"You don't have to be a psycho to want your picture," Gus replied.

"But it's unnerving when you know a psycho went to all of that trouble to get it," she replied.

Sam turned toward the detective. "Did you find out how he paid for it?"

"A ten-dollar bill came in the mail. One of the clerks remembers someone calling in and asking if it would be possible to buy a copy of the picture. She told him he could buy a copy of any picture in the files for ten dollars."

The doorbell chimed, and Sam walked across the room and flicked on the closed-circuit transistor television set that monitored the entrance below. Amelia Jones was framed in the tube. At her side was a large thin package wrapped in newsprint. "I'll be right down," Sam said in the intercom.

She did not say a word when she passed him the package, nor did she thank him for the hundred dollars he gave her, but her eyes suddenly brimmed with tears. She turned away and went out of the foyer. He followed her to the door and watched her climb into the right-hand side of a small pickup truck that was double-parked. A daisy was painted on the door panel. The light was too dim over the license plate to read it.

He waited until he was back upstairs and in the living room of the penthouse before he tore off the newsprint wrapping. Raquel had moved to the window and was staring out over the city. As the picture began to come into view, he turned it so that its back faced both of the women. It was a standing nude. The model stood with her legs apart, hands on her buttocks, pushing her hips forward. The dark mass of pubic hair was large, and it dominated the canvas so heavily that for a brief moment he did not see the face. The hair was blond and cut close to the head. The breasts were large, with erect nipples. Then the face held his attention. It was someone he had seen, but he could not place it.

Raquel turned from the window. "Well, let's see it, Sam." He hesitated.

"I'm a big girl, and so is Trudy."

He turned the picture around. Raquel's mouth fell open, her face reflecting sheer amazement. "Jesus Christ," she whispered presently. "It's Althea with a wig."

13

*S*OMEONE IN THE PROBATE COURT
had leaked to the press that there was a dispute over who was to be
named administrator of the Thurman estate. Sam, Trudy, and Raquel first heard of it over the radio in the taxicab that took them from
Sam's office to the probate court of the County of San Francisco, so
when they walked into the courtroom, they were not surprised to
find a heavy representation of the media, along with some fifty to
sixty spectators.

Howard Dredge and his two clients had already arrived.
Dredge appeared irritated, tapping his pince-nez nervously against
the knuckle of his left thumb. When he saw Sam, his lips pressed

themselves into a thin line of disapproval. The Colonel was in full uniform. He wore so many ribbons on the left breast of his tunic that they appeared as a rainbow patch. Althea sat to his right, slouched in her seat, shoulders hunched forward. She was as drab as a field mouse in her high-necked gray dress. Her hair was cropped masculine short, coming to a point on the nape of her neck. It was almost impossible to imagine such a drab creature posing with the wild abandon reflected in the portrait.

Judge Roland Novak also appeared displeased with the crowded courtroom as he came out of his chambers and sat down in his high-backed chair on the bench, but his admonition was mild. "This is a court of law," he said, "and I trust that judicial decorum will prevail. The issue at matter here today is to determine who shall be named administrator of the estate of the late Cyrus Thurman, Sr. There are two petitioners for this appointment by the court. One is Colonel Albert Thurman, and the other is Miss Raquel Thurman. If counsel for Colonel Thurman is prepared to state his case, we may proceed."

Howard Dredge cleared his throat and put on his pince-nez. "I would like to request that the courtroom be cleared of all persons other than witnesses, in view of the nature of the testimony that may be presented."

Judge Novak turned toward Sam Benedict. "Do you concur?"

"No, your Honor. We are well aware of the nature of the testimony, but we can think of no reason why this hearing should be held behind closed doors." Sam glanced toward the press table and saw Doug Kennedy of the *Chronicle* and Bill Montgomery of the *Examiner* scribbling in their notebooks. After all these years, Howard Dredge had not learned one of the basic rules of practical law—not to antagonize the press unnecessarily.

"The request is denied," the judge said. "You may proceed, Mr. Dredge."

The attorney frowned, and then called Mrs. Stella Ross. She was smartly dressed in a conservative knit suit, and she was thoroughly self-assured as she was sworn and assumed her place on the elevated witness chair.

"You are the mother of Colonel Albert Thurman?" Dredge asked.

"Yes."

"Is he your only child?"

"No. I had two others by a previous marriage."

Dredge again cleared his throat. "Is Colonel Albert Thurman the only issue of your marriage with the late Cyrus Thurman, Sr.?"

"He is."

Now Dredge took off his glasses and stared up at the ceiling of the courtroom. "Was this issue conceived naturally?"

"Naturally he was conceived."

Someone in the courtroom tittered, but it was quickly smothered when Judge Novak straightened in his chair.

"Let me rephrase the question," Dredge said, still staring at the ceiling. "Were any artificial means used to produce the pregnancy which resulted in the issue of your son, Colonel Albert Thurman?"

"No."

Dredge looked down from the ceiling. "Your witness," he said, glancing toward Sam.

"No questions."

Stella Ross stepped down from the stand without a glance toward her son and strode out of the courtroom.

"Mrs. Martha Myrick," Dredge said, and the bailiff repeated the name in a louder tone.

A large, stout woman, possibly in her early seventies, came from the back of the courtroom, was sworn, and took the stand. Her occupation was nurse and executive secretary, and she had retired from the staff of the Physicians and Surgeons Hospital some five years earlier. Dredge spent a very long time qualifying her as an authority on the procedures of the hospital. Sam finally interrupted to say that he would stipulate as to Mrs. Myrick's former employment and her qualifications.

Dredge pushed himself to his feet and walked toward the witness stand, carrying some papers in his hand. "Can you identify this?" he asked, giving one of the papers to her.

She glanced at it briefly. "It is a copy of the hospital record that notes the birth of a Raquel Dorothy Thurman, daughter of Cyrus Thurman and Dorothy Lorraine Thurman."

"This is a photocopy?"

"Yes."

"And did you type it?"

"I typed the original. It has my initials on the bottom of the page."

Dredge passed her another photocopy, and she went through the same routine of questions over the birth certificate of Cyrus Jr. The attorney, Sam noticed, had box hips, like a collie dog's. He gave his witness still another photostat. This time the elderly Mrs. Myrick raised her eyebrows when she read it. "Did you prepare this document?" Dredge asked.

The woman nodded slowly. "I believe I did. It also has my initials on the bottom of the page."

"And is this a receipt for payment in full for the artificial insemination of Mrs. Dorothy Lorraine Thurman on a date nine months and four days prior to the birth of Raquel Dorothy Thurman?"

"These are confidential records, and I—"

"Just answer the question, please, Mrs. Myrick."

She pursed her lips. "Yes, it is."

Dredge nodded and once again went through the same series

of questions concerning the impregnation of Dorothy Lorraine Thurman. The answers were the same, except Cyrus, Jr. was born six days short of the nine-month gestation period.

Sam sighed slowly. It was a mistake any young attorney might have made, but with an older lawyer, it was incredible. Dredge, however, was a corporation and tax lawyer. He probably had not been in court for years, but rare was the attorney who did not believe that he was an expert in court. Many coffins had been taken out of prisons because an accused had thought a corporation lawyer could as easily save him from the gas chamber as could the criminal specialist. He glanced briefly at the papers that Dredge brought over to him and raised no objection to their being introduced as evidence.

"Your witness," Dredge said with a pompous wave of his hand. He returned to his seat and sat down, then leaned to one side to accept some whispered words from the Colonel.

Sam leaned back in his chair and clasped his hands behind his head. "Did you keep a record as to the identity of the donor?" he asked mildly.

"No, I did not."

"Why not?"

Mrs. Myrick straightened. "Because this absolutely was most confidential," she replied indignantly. "No records as to the identity of a donor ever were made."

"That's all. Thank you very much." He leaned forward and began to doodle on his legal scratch pad, then glanced up toward the bench. Judge Novak had made a tent out of his hands and wore a thoughtful expression. At the other end of the long table, Dredge still listened to the whispering Colonel. "You may step down," Judge Novak said presently, and Dredge turned his attention back to the court.

Mrs. Myrick waddled from the witness stand back to her seat in the spectators' section of the courtroom.

If Dredge had listened to the cross-examination, he gave no indication of it. He rose, picked up some papers from the table, and approached the bench. "I do not have the original copy of the will in my possession," he said, "but I do have a photocopy of it." He passed a photocopy to the judge. "The court really has no other choice than to appoint Colonel Thurman as the administrator of the estate of the late Cyrus Thurman, Sr.," he said in his dry monotone. "Cyrus Thurman was most definite in expressing his wishes when he stated that he wanted the estate divided equally among the heirs of his body. There is only one heir of his body, namely Colonel Thurman. Neither Miss Raquel Thurman nor Cyrus Thurman, Jr., was an heir of his body. Cyrus Thurman, Jr., is deceased. Miss Raquel Thurman is not an heir of the late Cyrus Thurman, Sr.'s body. Evidence has established that she is the product of an artificial insemination. The evidence we have presented is virtually irrefutable in support of this. Thus, I respectfully petition this court to appoint Colonel Albert Thurman as the administrator of the estate of the late Cyrus Thurman, Sr."

He paused as Judge Novak picked up the copy of the will and began to read it.

Sam bent over as Trudy leaned toward him. "Aren't you going to point out that this phraseology was merely a popular form in use before the turn of the century?" she whispered.

Sam patted the back of her hand. Judge Novak put down the copy of the will and again looked thoughtfully toward Sam Benedict.

"I might add," Dredge continued, "that time is of the essence, as there is valuable property in the estate outside of the United States that should be conserved as quickly as possible." He pursed his lips, sat down, removed his glasses, and pinched his nose between his thumb and forefinger. The Colonel smiled and patted his attorney on the shoulder.

Sam leaned back in his chair and placed an ankle on his knee. "I would like to move that all the evidence concerning the alleged artificial insemination of the late Dorothy Lorraine Thurman be stricken as irrelevant. The sole issue here is to determine who shall be named as administrator of the estate."

Dredge turned around in his chair and looked at Sam, a puzzled expression on his face. Then he stood up. Judge Novak leaned forward in his high-backed chair. "What are you basing your motion upon?" he asked.

Sam ran his hand through his hair. "Testimony has been presented which proves that Cyrus Thurman was fertile," he said mildly. "Testimony has been presented which states there is no record in existence as to the identity of the donor," he said mildly. "No evidence has been presented to indicate that Cyrus Thurman, Sr., himself, indeed was *not* the donor."

Howard Dredge's mouth sagged open. He started to say something, then snapped his mouth shut and sat down.

"The motion is granted," Judge Novak said quietly.

Someone giggled, and Sam glanced quickly toward the other end of the table, and saw Althea bend forward and bury her face in her hands. Her shoulders shook, and her husband angrily put his hand on her shoulder, his fingers digging deep into the gray cloth. A stirring at the press table pulled Sam's attention away, and he watched the reporters writing rapidly, until Dredge once again stood up.

"If it please the court," Dredge said, nervously tapping his pince-nez in the palm of his hand, "this development was not anticipated, and I would like to ask for a continuance to some date at the court's convenience."

"May I ask the court for an adjournment only until this afternoon," Sam said quickly. "As Mr. Dredge pointed out earlier, time is of the essence, as we have a very valuable estate which needs to be preserved."

Judge Novak nodded. "Until two P.M.," he said.

Sam turned and whispered to Trudy, "Get Gus Corona and

have him come to my office as quickly as possible. Have Jack's send over some steak sandwiches and coffee." He turned back in his chair. Althea still sat with her face in her hands, but her shoulders no longer were shaking. The Colonel was staring at him malevolently, and Sam winked at him, then turned toward the reporters who were approaching his end of the long table.

The body taken from the waterfront had been brought to the morgue. It was that of a young woman, probably in her early twenties, and the cause of death was drowning. Very shortly before her death, however, she had suffered a severe blow, immediately above the right temple, which had fractured the skull and would have caused her to lose consciousness. Dental work, including a small bridge, was of European origin, and thus copies of the fingerprints that were taken from the body were sent to the United States Immigration Service. The victim was an Astrid Olson from Malmö, Sweden, who had arrived in San Francisco approximately two years earlier. Her sponsor had been a Colonel and Mrs. Albert Thurman. No missing-persons report had been filed. When the name "Thurman" appeared, a copy of the report was sent to Lieutenant Gus Corona, arriving on his desk shortly before noon.

There had been another series of reports that intrigued Corona. Raymond Saxeby had left his home at the usual time, but he had proceeded only a few blocks before he had turned and gone back to his house. He had remained inside for approximately an hour, then had emerged carrying two large suitcases, which he had placed in the trunk of his car. Next he had driven aimlessly around the Sunset District for about a half-hour before he drove directly to the courthouse. Here he had asked for directions to the probate court. During the remainder of the morning he had been a spectator at the Thurman hearing. The last report placed him in a small restaurant near the courthouse, drinking beer and eating a grilled cheese sandwich.

Sam drank his second cup of coffee and listened quietly as Corona brought up the latest developments. "A search warrant to go through Saxeby's garage probably will be issued this afternoon," the detective said. "It's getting harder every day to get a search warrant. Some of the judges shudder every time we ask for one."

"Whatever he had in his garage is now probably in his suitcase," Sam commented. "And what I don't understand is his interest in the Thurmans."

"Well, whatever the reason, he's certainly interested."

Sam nodded. "There may be a little excitement in Judge Novak's court this afternoon, Gus. I think it would be a good idea if you had some plainclothesmen strategically spotted around the courtroom. I'm going to be a little rough on the upright Colonel, and unless he comes up with some convincing answers, he may come apart."

"What are you going to do?"

"I can't say right at the moment. Everything depends on the answers he gives."

"It hardly seems possible," Raquel said quietly. "Albert is avaricious, insufferable, and vain. But he also is a very proper person, and I cannot see him doing anything that would not be considered proper."

"You may be right," Sam replied. He then poured himself another cup of coffee and proceeded to sip it slowly as Gus Corona picked up the telephone.

The courtroom was still crowded for the afternoon session when Sam and Raquel returned shortly before two. Dredge and the two other Thurmans had already arrived, and the attorney and the Colonel were at their end of the table whispering, their heads close together. Sam found Saxeby with little difficulty as they walked through the spectators. He was the only man in the room with white crew-cut hair. He sat on the edge of the aisle, legs crossed, hands cupped across one knee. When Sam turned to sit down, he noticed that the man was staring at Raquel. Most men stared at his client, but there was another factor in the look Saxeby fastened upon her. The eyes expressed a helpless yearning, somewhat like a puppy who knows he has done something wrong and is quietly seeking forgiveness and affection at the same time.

A uniformed bailiff came in from a side door, walked importantly over to the court clerk, then, tucking his thumbs in his belt, turned to survey the crowd. Presently his eyebrows raised slightly, and Sam turned slowly in his chair to see what had caused the reaction. Gus Corona was leaning against one of the walls, talking quietly to a heavyset man with a large stomach who was a cartoonist's caricature of a cop. The man turned, and Sam recognized the man as Lars Burton. When Sam turned back, the bailiff was disappearing into the judge's chambers. A few minutes later the bailiff returned and stood beside the bench, his arms folded across his chest.

Judge Novak came out of his chambers with a frown. He pursed his lips, walked directly to his chair, and banged his gavel twice. When the murmur had subsided, he leaned back in his chair and formed his hands into a tent. "The purpose of this hearing is to determine solely whom the court will appoint as the administrator of the estate of the late Cyrus Thurman, Sr." His eyes rested first on Sam Benedict, then Howard Dredge, and then flickered around the courtroom. They came to a stop on Althea. "There will be no smoking while court is in session," he said. Althea crushed her cigarette into an ashtray on the table.

Howard Dredge stood up. "I would like to make an observation to the court that the entire principle of artificial insemination is based upon the theory that such a procedure is brought into practice only when the husband is impotent."

"I object," Sam said mildly. "On the grounds—"

"Sustained. The court has already ruled upon this, Mr. Dredge."

Dredge sighed. "I call Colonel Thurman."

The Colonel was indeed a military man. He stood as straight as a plank when he was sworn in, and he sat straight in the chair. His voice was brusque and clipped when he identified himself in response to Dredge's questions. He had been born in San Francisco, attended San Francisco State College "before it became overrun with hippies," and enlisted in the Army. But because of his high IQ he had been sent at once to Officer Candidate School, where he naturally emerged with a commission. During his military career he had served as a procurement officer, dealing with accounts running in excess of one million dollars; finance officer; many times a commanding officer; and provost marshal.

Sam made a mental note.

"How long have you known your sister, Miss Raquel Thurman?" Dredge asked.

"Ever since she was born."

"From many years' observation, have you ever noticed anything in her character that would qualify her to handle such—"

"I object," Sam said. "The witness has not been qualified as a psychiatrist."

"Sustained."

"She has always been a frivolous girl. She dabbles in interior—"

"The objection was sustained," the judge said quietly.

"Do you believe that your many years' experience in dealing with vast sums of the taxpayers' money and your integrity as a high-ranking officer in the United States Army qualify you to successfully perform the role of administrator of your late father's estate?"

"Of course. Otherwise I would not be here."

"Have you had any other experience in managing fiscal affairs outside of your Army activities?"

"Yes. My wife inherited a rather sizable amount from her father. By careful investment I have increased the size of her estate dramatically, and, I might mention, I took a prominent part in settling her father's estate."

"Your witness," Dredge said as he squeezed his square hips into his chair.

Sam stood up and leaned against the table. "Do you live off your wife's inheritance?" he asked casually.

The Colonel's eyes narrowed. "Other than the fact that we live in her family home, I have never touched one cent of hers in my life."

Althea glanced toward her husband for the first time, straightened in her chair, and folded her arms across her chest.

"Whose funds maintain the operation of the house?"

"Mine," the Colonel snapped.

"Does that include the maid?"

The Colonel folded his hands. "It is my wife's personal maid, a luxury for which she pays out of her own funds."

"What happened to her?"

The Colonel looked at him with a puzzled expression.

"I object on the grounds that—" Dredge said, standing up.

"I'll connect it up," Sam said quickly.

Judge Novak paused. "I'll withhold ruling," he said.

"What happened to her, the maid, Astrid Olson?" Out of the corner of his eye Sam saw the press gallery growing more alert. Dredge sat down.

"She went to Los Angeles to visit a friend."

"How long ago?"

"Several days ago."

"Could it possibly have been on the day of your father's murder?"

Dredge leaped from his chair. His pince-nez fell from his nose and dangled on the end of a thin black ribbon. "This is outrageous."

Judge Novak looked speculatively toward Sam Benedict, then

glanced around the courtroom once again. "I said earlier that the purpose of this hearing was to determine whom the court would appoint as an administrator."

"I can assure the court that this is related directly to the matter at hand," Sam said. "We are interested in determining the qualifications of two persons, namely, which is the better. I can assure the court that this will be connected up."

Judge Novak nodded. "Go ahead," he said.

Sam repeated the question.

"No."

"Was it the day after the murder?"

"I believe it was."

"Did you know that yesterday the body of your maid, Miss Astrid Olson, was found floating in San Francisco Bay?"

The Colonel opened and closed his mouth several times in rapid succession, but his back remained as straight as ever. His eyes reflected no emotion, however, nor did they waver from Sam's. "No, I did not," he said. Then slowly his fingers began to drum a slow and silent tattoo on his knee.

"Did your father call you from Mexico two days before he was murdered and tell you that he was planning to change his will?"

"No."

"Did he call you?"

"No, he did not." The Colonel had the words out before Dredge could voice another objection.

Sam Benedict rocked slowly back and forth in his chair. Then he stood up, walked over to the court clerk, and picked up the two receipts for the payment of the artificial insemination. "These are exhibits D and E," he said mildly.

Howard Dredge interrupted. "The court has already ruled that the artificial insemination of Dorothy Lorraine Thurman is beyond the scope of this hearing," he said. "This is harassment, pure and simple."

"I am not referring at all to the artificial insemination," Sam said in his same deceptively mild tone. "I refer to the receipts."

The judge suddenly assumed a thoughtful look. "Go on," he said, straightening in his chair.

Sam turned back to the Colonel. "You have seen these before?" he asked.

"Of course," he snapped. "They were gathered when we were preparing for this hearing."

"And where did you gather them from?"

"My wife is the granddaughter of Mr. Beldon, who for many years was a prominent attorney in San Francisco," the Colonel said icily. "She not only worked in his office on occasion, but after his death, she took some of his personal files to our home to help in the settlement of his estate. Mr. Beldon, as you probably know, drew up the will for my late father, and there is no question in my mind but what my father knew exactly what he was doing when he had the will drawn up in the manner in which it was."

"What are these two documents?" Sam said patiently.

"They are receipts for the artificial insemination of my father's second wife."

"They are photocopies of receipts. Am I correct?"

"Yes, you are correct."

Sam turned to Judge Novak. "If the court please, may I interrupt the cross-examination of the witness to call another? I would like to reserve the right to call Colonel Thurman back to the stand."

"Granted." Judge Novak nodded his head. "You may step down, Colonel."

Sam turned to the clerk and asked him to call Lieutenant Gus Corona, who, with a faintly surprised look, came from the back of the room and was sworn.

Dredge whispered to the Colonel, who responded by a swift shaking of his head.

"You are attached to the Homicide Division of the San Francisco Police Department?"

"I am."

"Are you presently investigating the murder of the late Cyrus Thurman, Sr.?"

"I am."

"During the course of this investigation, did you examine the personal effects of the deceased, which were left at the home of Miss Raquel Thurman?"

"I did."

Sam picked up exhibits D and E once again and showed them to the detective. "Have you seen the originals of these copies?"

Gus Corona studied them for a moment, then nodded. "Yes," he said. "The originals were in a suitcase belonging to the deceased that was taken from the home of Miss Raquel Thurman and later replaced."

Dredge jumped to his feet once again. "Your Honor, I must protest this character assassination by innuendo." He waved his arm toward the reporters' table. "Counsel is trying this case in the press, and I can see no relevancy to this line of questioning other than for sensationalism."

Judge Novak leaned forward. "I'll still withhold the ruling," he said. "But I assume that counsel for Miss Raquel Thurman will very shortly connect this line."

"Yes, I will, your Honor." Sam turned back to the detective as Dredge reluctantly sank back in his seat. "That is all."

"No questions," Dredge said.

Colonel Albert Thurman was showing his anger when he went back to the stand. Again he sat straight as a board, feet slightly apart and planted firmly on the floor.

Sam passed him the photostats. "Do you have any knowledge when these copies were made?"

"I do not. It obviously was before Mr. Beldon died, or they

would not have been in his files. The mere fact that they were in his files makes it apparent that my father intended precisely what he meant to say when the will was drawn up."

Sam nodded. "I call your attention to the border of the photostats. You will notice that the paper on which the copies were made is somewhat larger than the original documents."

"You are very observant," the Colonel said sarcastically.

Sam ignored the comment. "I call your attention to the fact that a seal has been pressed into this blank space on the paper," he said. "I wonder if you would read to the court the words that are impressed into this blank space."

The Colonel took a pair of glasses from his pocket and held the paper up in front of him. "It says 'Martin Grossbeck, Photos.' " He lowered the paper.

"What else does it say, Colonel? Read it in its entirety."

The Colonel pursed his lips and once again raised the photostat. " 'Martin Grossbeck, Photos, 220 Fox Plaza, San Francisco, California,' " he said. He lowered the paper; then suddenly a look of absolute bewilderment flooded his face.

"Precisely," Sam said. "The Fox Plaza wasn't built until just a few years ago, and that was long after Mr. Beldon died. So how did these photostats get into the personal files of Mr. Beldon?"

The Colonel suddenly sagged, and he looked across at his wife. She had straightened in her chair, and now she began to giggle, burying her face in her hands. Two reporters stood up and began moving out of the room. The movement started a murmur of voices throughout the spectators' section. Judge Novak picked up his gavel and rapped it sharply. The sound stopped Althea's giggles. She dropped her hands and looked up, first toward the judge, then her husband, and finally toward the two reporters who had paused by the rail. Slowly she bent down, picked up her purse, and placed it in her lap. As she fumbled with the catch, Sam lunged toward her, knocking Dredge from his chair, and seized her by both wrists at the moment she pulled out a small ball-peen hammer. Then suddenly she began screaming and kicking at him for what seemed an eternity, until the bailiff and one of the detectives reached his side and pulled her away.

14

---

*W*HEN THE SCUFFLE had first
started, Raymond Saxeby was the first person in the spectators' section to jump to his feet. For a brief second he had started to move up
toward the bench; then he had paused as Gus Corona brushed past
him while running to the front of the courtroom. Lars Burton noticed that Saxeby's reactions had been contagious, for everyone in the
courtroom now was standing, ignoring the continuous banging of
Judge Novak's gavel and his ineffectual cries for order. His eyes
flickered steadily between Raquel Thurman, who sat at the end of
the lawyers' table with her fingers pressed against her lips, and the
Colonel, who had not moved from the witness chair. Then Saxeby

turned and walked rapidly out of the courtroom. He had a peculiar walk, Burton noticed for the first time. He glided, his body not moving up and down at all. He stepped aside as two sheriff's deputies burst in the door, then slipped out into the corridor before the doors swung shut.

The Colonel's wife had been restrained, and her screams had turned into obscene and hysterical cries of rage. Lars Burton slowly drifted toward the door. It pushed open again, and another deputy stepped inside, then stood in front of it with his arms folded across his chest. "Wait a minute, mister."

"Burton, Homicide," he replied, fishing out his badge.

The deputy glanced at it and became friendly. "What's going on?"

"Sam Benedict caught another one in the courtroom," he replied. "She blew her stack."

"He'd make a good cop."

Burton put his hand to his mouth as he belched. "I don't think there is enough money in it for him," he replied, moving past the deputy.

A crowd was gathering in the hall, and those in front tried to see in beyond the deputy who guarded the other side of the door. There was no sign of Saxeby.

The detective walked slowly to his car, slid behind the wheel, and popped another antacid tablet into his mouth before he started the engine and turned on the radio. Saxeby had driven out of the parking lot and was driving up Van Ness. He was driving fast. Lars Burton once again began to trail the surveillance cars. Thoughts moved randomly through his mind. Althea Thurman probably would never stand trial. She surely didn't like her old man. Nutty broad. Someday Benedict would pull one of his courtroom deals and get shot. He sure had shaken up the probate court today. It was the most action old Judge Novak had probably seen in ten years. Sam Benedict could be wrong. There had to be some reason, or some connection, between the psycho they were following and the nutty broad in the courtroom. He thought of the report Corona had written earlier about her posing for and banging her brother-in-law and everyone else in Creep Alley. Maybe the two psychos had been banging each other in some nuthouse somewhere.

"He's gone into the Marina District again," the radio reported. "He was burning rubber on the last turn."

Burton picked up the microphone. "Enough to pick him up on a violation?"

"Marginal."

What was his goddamn hurry? It probably was something in the stars that told him to drive fast on Thursday. If they picked him up on a traffic violation, however, they could get a chance to find out what he was carrying in those suitcases. He reached for the microphone to call for a traffic car, then paused when the radio reported that Saxeby had parked in the area outside of the Yacht Club. A moment later the surveillance team reported that Saxeby had opened the trunk and then a suitcase inside the trunk. Then they had moved past him in order not to attract his attention. "He's walking away very fast."

Lars Burton increased his speed. The second trail car moved up. "He's moving at a half-run up the street," the radio reported. "Something's on his mind."

A bus pulled out from the curb, and Burton was forced to brake and swerve widely to avoid hitting it. The microphone fell into his lap.

"Now he's running," the radio said. "But we don't think he spotted us. He's just turning the corner."

Burton, swearing silently, recovered the microphone. "Pick him up," he ordered, his voice giving no indication of his anger. "He's probably armed."

For two or three minutes the radio was silent but for the static; then once again the flat voice came back through the speaker.

"He went into a house before we could get to him. It's a large white house, the fourth from the corner. He fumbled at the lock before he went in, so it looks like a forced entry."

The detective recalled the cheap snap lock with the wide aperture on the Thurman home.

"Do you want us to go in after him?"

"Not now." Again he sighed. "But cover the front and the back and grab him if he comes out. Keep out of his sight now." A few minutes later he pulled up beside Saxeby's shabby sedan in the parking lot by the seawall.

He opened the trunk of Saxeby's car with a master key. The larger of the two suitcases had been left unlatched. Among a pile of dirty clothes was a bloodstained leather jacket and a white lace bra and white blouse, both also stained with blood. Small squares had been scissored from each of the three garments, and Lars Burton knew where the missing swatches were—in the evidence room at police headquarters, where they had been locked after being turned over by the newspapers. Burton called for more help, then cordoned off the block, making sure that none of the police could be seen from the house. He went back to Saxeby's car and forced the latch on the second suitcase. It contained nothing but clothing and some astrological charts carefully folded on the bottom, but glued to the lid of the suitcase was the picture of Raquel Thurman. It no longer was a regular eight-by-ten photograph, however. The edges had been cut away to form the shape of a Valentine-card heart.

Five hours later Gus Corona and Lars Burton sat together in a police car just around the corner from the Thurman residence. It was just a matter of waiting. A command post had been set up in the parking area adjacent to the Yacht Club. A plainclothesman had been installed in a house diagonally across from the Thurman residence, where he could watch the front. Two men covered the rear.

"We're going to have to go in after him," Burton said for about the twentieth time.

"Let's wait a little longer. Sometimes these guys don't have unlimited patience."

The radio sputtered softly; then a voice came on the special frequency. "Sam Benedict is down here and wants to know if you would like some company."

"I haven't had a chance to talk to him since lunch," Corona replied. "Tell him where we are parked and ask him to come up."

"That's a good idea," Lars Burton said. "We can send him right up to the door, and he can talk Saxeby into coming out."

Corona chuckled. "He might just be able to."

"Someday Benedict is going to get killed. If that broad today had had a gun instead of a hammer, he might of got it then."

Corona shook his head. "Sam Benedict is as quick on his feet as he is in his head."

The rear door of the police car opened, and Lars Burton turned in his seat as Sam Benedict slid in. He had changed his clothes since his fight in the courtroom and looked as dapper as ever. "Come after another client?" Burton asked.

Sam shook his head. "Hardly. Saxeby still in there?"

Corona nodded. "What's happening on the other front? Nobody tells us anything when we are out in the field."

"They are holding Althea Thurman on suspicion of murder in the prison ward. There is blood on the hammer she was carrying that matched that of the Olson girl."

"She cop out?"

"They gave her a shot in the courtroom, and the last I heard, she was still out. Her husband was hanging around for a while trying to see her, but he finally gave up."

"Where is the Colonel now?"

"I don't know."

"If my wife was out balling a bunch of hippies and had the same opinion of me that Mrs. Thurman had of her husband, I don't think I'd want to talk to her," Burton said.

"He said he felt sorry for her, that he had known she was deteriorating mentally," Sam said. "He told the police also that the Olson girl used to go down every night to sleep on his boat."

"And so the Olson girl made the trip at the wrong time of night this time," Burton said tiredly.

The radio squawked again. Colonel Albert Thurman was at the roadblock and was demanding that he be allowed to pass.

"Is he aware of the situation?" Corona asked.

"Ten-four, but he still wants to come through. As a matter of fact, he is demanding it."

"Why don't you have him come up as far as we are," Sam said mildly. "Maybe we could explain the situation a little better."

Burton took out his roll of tablets and popped another one in his mouth, as Corona told the command post to send the Colonel up to the car. He remembered the look that Thurman had thrown Benedict when he was under cross-examination and wondered if it might not be practical to exchange seats with the lawyer.

"It was very foggy that night," Sam said. "The night Cy was murdered."

"Yeah," Burton agreed. "It was foggy." He turned once again toward the attorney. Corona raised his foot up on the seat and also faced the lawyer.

"The two kids didn't hear the woman scream until after they had sideswiped the car. If it was the Olson girl screaming, maybe she was killed on the boat," Sam Benedict continued.

"That'll be checked, Sam," Corona said. "You didn't come all the way out here just to tell us that."

"No," the lawyer said. "Let's remember what else the kids heard, then be very quiet and listen."

For a brief moment there was only the sound of the three of them breathing, and then Burton heard the sharp and brisk click of military heels slapping the pavement behind the police car. As they

174

grew closer, he heard a metallic sound, the sound made by metal cleats built into heels. Corona suddenly swore softly and loosened his jacket. Lars Burton felt a sudden dull pain in his stomach. The steps grew closer, and Burton eased his gun from the holster. The steps paused for a split second, as Gus Corona slowly opened the door of the car; then the metallic clack increased tempo, passed behind the car, and started across the road. Lars Burton moved quickly, opening his door and sliding out of the seat. "Over here, Colonel," he said. He could see the man hesitate again before he broke into a run, his feet slamming the pavement hard. Before Burton was halfway across the street, his quarry had disappeared around the corner.

Burton ran. Christ, how he hated to run. It made his stomach hurt and his heart pound. Corona moved faster, passing him, then veering off to the left to split a possible target. As he turned the corner, Burton heard a shot, saw the man ahead of him lurch, and at the same time saw his duck-billed cap fly into the air. The man still kept running, however, although now he was in a crouch, weaving as he ran.

The front door of the Thurman home suddenly opened wide, and Lars abruptly came to a stop. In the dark, he could barely make out the shadow in the doorway. A gunshot came from the doorway, and a bullet ricocheted with a wild scream off into the night. Lars raised his arm, aimed carefully, and squeezed the trigger. A split second later he heard another shot to his left. The shadow in the doorway doubled over, and then snapped back as if he were a puppet on a string.

The Colonel had reached the first step of the stairs. Gus Corona, running hard, cut sharply across the street, angling in. "Thurman," Lars yelled. "Stop or you are a dead man."

The Colonel hesitated, and Lars once again squeezed the trigger of his revolver, placing the shot just ahead of Thurman. He turned, placed his hands on his hips, and stood with legs apart. Slowly

Lars Burton moved toward the house. A couple of blocks away sirens suddenly began to moan, and he became aware of red lights reflecting in the sky. Corona moved in to his left, still staying wide.

"You take the Colonel?" Corona said mildly.

"Imbeciles," Thurman shouted, then turned and started up the stairs again.

"You want to die?" Burton said angrily. "Just take one more step." He held his revolver straight out stiffly. "Clasp your hands behind your head."

The Colonel whirled around, saw the two revolvers, then slowly raised his hands. Burton was close enough to see the hate reflected in Thurman's eyes, but he said nothing, his mouth pressed in a straight line. Black-and-white cars suddenly squealed around both corners of the block, and one pulled up in front of the driveway.

"No, I'll take the psycho," Burton said to Corona. He eased past the Colonel and went up the stairs, his gun still pointed ahead of him.

Raymond Saxeby lay on his back amid the wreckage of a small antique table in the foyer of the house. His revolver lay on the carpet a good three feet away from his outstretched arm. His waist was covered with blood, and he was breathing heavily. Burton saw Saxeby's eyes follow him as he moved past the outstretched feet and kicked the revolver farther away. "You're safe," Saxeby said hoarsely. "I'm paralyzed. I can't move nothing."

"We'll get an ambulance," Burton replied quietly.

Two uniformed men warily came in the door, and Burton told one to watch Saxeby and for the other to call for the ambulance. Then he went back down the stairs. Thurman was standing stiffly against the wall of the house, hands on his hips, his face flushed.

"He's clean," Gus Corona said.

Burton put his gun away and belched. He reached for an antacid tablet, but he had left them in the car. When he realized this, his stomach began to ache again. "I think I got an ulcer or something," he said to Corona.

"You'll have a lot more than an ulcer when I get through with you," Thurman shouted.

Burton ignored him. "I'll take a look around inside."

"Not without a search warrant, you don't," the Colonel screamed.

Neither detective paid any attention. Corona signaled a uniformed sergeant, then nodded toward the enraged Colonel. "Albert Thurman," he said mildly. "Take him down and book him on suspicion of murder."

The Colonel's mouth sagged. His shoulders slumped and presently he began to cry.

15

---

*I*T WAS TOO LATE at night, or rather too early in the morning, to be explaining, but Raquel and Trudy were still up when Sam returned to his penthouse with Gus Corona. Raquel looked very tired. Her shoulders slumped, and there were dark circles under her eyes.

"We saw a lot of it on television," Trudy said, making them a drink. She appeared as fresh as she did in the morning when she arrived in the office.

"Saxeby is the most talkative," Gus Corona said after a while. "He says he knows he will die shortly because the stars so indicate. He says he cast another horoscope last night, and there was only one thing he could do. So he did it."

"There's no doubt that he is the Astro killer?"

"None at all," the detective continued. "He's confessed to

twelve murders, which is more than we thought, but in his first slayings he didn't notify the newspapers. He says there had to be a sacrifice for each sun sign. He says this was written in his horoscope. If he had been successful in getting the Colonel, this would have been thirteen. He says he went after the Colonel because of his love for you."

Raquel shuddered. "How could he?" she asked softly.

Corona swirled the ice cubes around in his glass. "It's rather interesting the way Saxeby phrases it," he continued. "When he read in the papers that he was being blamed for killing your father, he became furious because this was a murder of which he was innocent. According to his way of thinking, the other killings were not crimes. They were astrological sacrifices. When he saw your picture in the papers, the stars told him that as soon as he got rid of your father's murderer, who to Saxeby was an outrageous impostor, then you would be his mate."

"He's very talkative," Sam said speculatively.

"He's going to die," Corona replied. "He says the stars indicate he will die within the next twenty-four hours. The doctors say they might pull him through if he had a will to live but that the will is missing."

"It will save three years or more of litigation," Sam said.

"Of course," Gus agreed. "But to be charitable, Sam, he may have saved your life. That night the Colonel was shooting at you in Sausalito, Saxeby was parked in the driveway of an empty house in back of the Colonel waiting for you to come home. The stars had told him that was a good night to meet you. He tried to call you. In fact, he had tried several times, once apparently when I answered." The detective held his glass out to Trudy for another drink and nodded his thanks when she stood up and took it to the bar. "When the Colonel started to chase you down the hill, he chased the Colonel and bumped him sufficiently hard to make him sideswipe the cliff. "He's

179

very proud of his actions that night. He goes into great detail of how he followed the Colonel to Tiburon and watched him leave the Kevin car and go to his own carrying the rifle."

"If he was planning to kill the Colonel, why didn't he do it then?" Trudy asked, passing him his drink.

"The stars were not right. He says he didn't know who the Colonel was until he recognized him in court. He says also he didn't know whether the Colonel was after Raquel or Sam until today."

Raquel rose to her feet and walked over to the glass doors to look out over the city. "Who was Albert after?" she asked presently.

"Probably both of you," Gus replied. "The Colonel is still indignant."

"Albert killed Daddy, didn't he?"

"There doesn't seem to be much doubt about it. In his bedroom closet we found a rifle and a revolver. Ballistics says the revolver is the one that killed your father, and the rifle is the one used to shoot at you and Sam."

"But why?" Raquel turned away from the window, then added, "He must be as mad as Saxeby."

Corona placed his drink on the coffee table and lit a cigarette. "We have a taped statement from Althea Thurman also," he said.

Raquel came back from the patio doors and sat down. "Is she going to be all right?"

"The doctors say she will recover."

For a moment there was silence. Then Raquel looked from Sam to Trudy and back to the detective. "I'm a big girl," she said presently. "What did she have to say? Let's get it all over with now."

"It wasn't too coherent," Corona said. "She hated the Colonel, and the Colonel hated her. She not only had Junior for her stud, but she told the Colonel she had chosen him because she knew her husband disliked him intensely."

"She's as sick as the others." Raquel shivered. "Why didn't they just divorce?"

"According to her, he wouldn't leave her because of her money and because a couple of his superior officers disapproved of divorce. This is where she rambled. She says in one place that she was a late bloomer and in another that she never was going to live out the rest of her life as a spinster. But most of her statement is rational, and it ties up the Colonel tightly. She goes into great detail about the money he owed her. Every time he borrowed from her, she made him sign a promissory note with interest. He borrowed heavily, taking long gambles. He lost on wildcat oil ventures, the corn-futures market, even the penny stockmarket. Over the years he had become indebted to her for almost a million dollars, exclusive of interest. All the notes were due when he inherited his share of his father's estate." Gus leaned forward and stubbed out his cigarette in an ashtray. "Althea giggled when she told how shocked her husband was when his father called and said he was returning to San Francisco to change his will."

"How does she tie him into the murder?" Sam asked.

"Beautifully. About three-quarters of an hour before Cy Senior was scheduled to arrive at the Colonel's house, the Colonel went outside for a walk. He was wearing a leather bush jacket. He returned a little after midnight wearing a pullover sweater that he kept on the boat. About a half-hour after the Colonel had left the house, the maid, Astrid Olson, left the house to spend the night on the boat. Apparently the Olson girl liked to sleep there. The following morning, when the maid didn't show up to work, Althea went down to the boat. The flight bag in which the maid carried her nightgown and other things was on the boat. The leather jacket, very wet, was hanging in the head. She brought it back to the house."

"Did she ask him about it?"

"Apparently not. I don't think they communicated very much. She hung the jacket in a kitchen closet, went into the den, and saw her husband, who then told her about Cy's murder," Gus continued. "The Colonel left the house shortly after this and returned about two hours later carrying a suitcase, which he put in the garage. His knuckles were cut. When he went out again, she went down to the garage. It was a black Samsonite case with clothing for a middle-aged man inside of it."

"She didn't report it?" Raquel asked incredulously.

"She's not very bright. She says she did not become suspicious of her husband until the police started looking for the maid," Gus said. "Only then did she go back to the boat. This time she found the ball-peen hammer with blood on it. It was in the empty bait tank. She says that the entire picture came to her in court today and that she was taking out the hammer to show it, not use it as a weapon, when she lost control and Sam restrained her. Burton took Cy's suitcase out to the hospital. Althea has identified the case and the contents as the one her husband brought home the day after the murder of the elder Thurman. He probably killed Junior when he went after the suitcase, and the maid because he did not expect that she would be on the boat, and she saw him with his bloodstained coat."

"I told Junior not to answer the telephone," Raquel said flatly. "If he had answered the phone, then maybe Albert wouldn't have gone out there."

Sam shook his head. "Either way, he would have gone," he said. "He wanted to see the changes in the will."

Raquel frowned. "I don't understand why he took the suit-case *back* to my house," she said.

"Possibly he wanted the original copy of the will to show up," Sam speculated. "And there was no way he could be sure that the police hadn't thoroughly searched your house."

"The woman the two kids heard screaming was the maid," Gus said.

Raquel went over to the bar and poured a small glass of Dry Sack sherry.

Corona watched her. "Saxeby had a letter in his jacket pocket that was addressed to you. It was a very poorly written love letter."

"Throw it away."

"We have to keep it," the detective said. "It was written on the same typewriter that wrote the letters to the newspapers. It was in his garage, which he had turned into some sort of a temple."

Raquel remained by the bar, holding the wine glass. "What did the letter say?"

"That he loved you and that astrologically you were destined to be mates. It says something about Mercury going backward and that he would see you in the next life on Uranus, or something like that."

She tipped the glass up and drained it, then placed it very carefully on the bar. "Will you take me home, Gus?"

"Right now?"

She nodded. "I just want to go home."

A few moments after they had left, Trudy brought another drink to where Sam was standing by the patio doors. The fog was blowing in again, coming in fast like a winter snowstorm, and half the city was already shrouded. "There are a couple of things I don't understand, Sam," she said, standing beside him. "Why did Albert try to kill you and Raquel in Sausalito if he already thought he had the estate on the legal technicality?"

Sam shook his head. "I don't know, Trudy. During our conference he made a reference to lawyers looting the estate. He probably thought that our demise would be a more direct solution to the problem."

For a long moment they watched the fog; then Trudy said, "I always worry over you, Sam, but I guess you are safe for this night. Will you take me home now?"

He slipped his arm around her waist. "I don't have a car. You had better go to bed and risk a ruined reputation."

The telephone rang. Trudy slipped away from him and picked it up. "May I tell him what it is about?" she asked. A moment

183

later, she placed her hand over the mouthpiece. "It's a lieutenant from police headquarters. He says Colonel Thurman has asked you to represent him." She shook her head. "Shall I tell him that there is a conflict of interest?"

Sam nodded. "A decided conflict of interest," he replied.